Praise for *The Whale's Last Song*

'An exquisite story threaded through with heart and compassion, underpinned by immense wisdom, insight and hope ... a bright ode to all that is good and beautiful in the world. *The Whale's Last Song* is a timeless tale, an allegory of the heart' – Maggie Hamilton, *When We Become Strangers*

'Joanne's writing is beautiful. *The Whale's Last Song* is a fresh, exquisite fictional work. It is a creative tour de force of an idea, born in a phase of Joanne's life a few months after she lost her beloved mother ... It is a piece of art which involves the reader in a new world and a new way of seeing. Both challenging and reassuring, the story weaves a sense of belonging through the fallibility of being human and the mysteries of being alive' – Suzie Miller, *Prima Facie*

The Whale's Last Song

Joanne Fedler is an internationally bestselling author, writing mentor and women's rights activist. Her books have sold over 750,000 copies worldwide. She is an open-water ocean swimmer with a special love of whales, Port Jackson sharks and turtles. *The Whale's Last Song* is her fifteenth book.

For dearest
Dalya
May this little story
land gently in your heart,
like a splash, a whisper.
I wish you whales —
and song
and ducklings

The Whale's Last Song

JOANNE FEDLER

With love
Joanne

FOURTH ESTATE

Fourth Estate
An imprint of HarperCollins*Publishers*

HarperCollins*Publishers*
Australia • Brazil • Canada • France • Germany • Holland • India
Italy • Japan • Mexico • New Zealand • Poland • Spain • Sweden
Switzerland • United Kingdom • United States of America

HarperCollins acknowledges the Traditional Custodians
of the lands upon which we live and work, and pays respect
to Elders past and present.

First published on Gadigal Country in Australia in 2024
by HarperCollins*Publishers* Australia Pty Limited
ABN 36 009 913 517
harpercollins.com.au

A catalogue record for this book is available from the National Library of Australia

ISBN 978 1 4607 6600 2 (hardback)
ISBN 978 1 4607 1755 4 (ebook)

Cover design by Hazel Lam, HarperCollins Design Studio
Cover images by istockphoto.com
Internal images: fork (p172–173), cockroach (p216), mouse (p216), tree (p249),
whale (p251), feather (p273) and wind gust dinkus by shutterstock.com. All other
illustrations by Joanne Fedler.
Epigraph quotation on page xiii from *The Leaf And The Cloud* by Mary Oliver,
copyright © 2000. Reprinted by permission of Da Capo Press, an imprint of
Hachette Book Group, Inc.
Author photograph by Danielle Minett, Natural Light Photography
Typeset in Bembo Std by Kirby Jones
Printed and bound in Australia by McPherson's Printing Group

For my own mama
who made me a little girl again
when Life took her back

'A full life is a beautiful life – although it can also be a difficult, even tragic life.'
– Andreas Weber

'Whatever you do will be insignificant, but it is very important that you do it.'
– Unattributed

'Maybe the world, without us, is the real poem.'
– Mary Oliver

Before Our Story Begins

There was a time when the forests and the mountains and the sloping woods belonged to no human. The world was a pulsing heart, and each small thing knew its place in this grand scheme, without which, the whole machine of it would stop, and all that lived, would die.

There was enough of everything – warmth, clouds, rain, fruit and nuts. Kindness from one person to another flowed easily, and between people and animals and trees and flowers and weeds. Everything knew its place: the worms knew how to do their worm-work, the bees did their bee-business, and the butterflies were the most delicate ambassadors of hope and change.

Every day knew it was new; not the same as yesterday nor the same as tomorrow. People woke from their dreams and beheld the dawn, and their first utterance was to thank the new day for coming back again. There was none of this 'taking for granted' business, or expecting a morning to arrive on time, like a job that begins at 7 am sharp – and if you're late again tomorrow that will be your final warning.

Every person understood that to be human was to carry the responsibility of completing creation. No-one was exempt nor wished to be excused, like one might try to writhe out of conscription for a war you did not want to fight in. No, this was a time long before men found ways to cull their young by leaving battlefields bloodied with their beautiful, fragile strength, strewn for the vultures and jackals, to return to the dust.

And what a curious notion to imagine you were exceptional or special or, even more preposterously, *chosen*, and could do it alone. It would have been as ludicrous as thinking love was a private enterprise, something you could do all by yourself.

No-one questioned this core truth nor felt burdened by the duty of it. To serve your part was to lighten yourself. The more you gave away, the lighter you became. And lightness was the purpose for which all beings were made. Everything appreciated this.

So when did it happen that people started to forget?

The Great Forgetting began when humans built walls to keep the wild at bay, as if they had not emerged from and of its slushy, mucky, heaving chaos. Their thinking turned to splitting and splicing, and it spread and mutated like a virus. Soon all things were hacked, divided and othered; the world separated into human and inhuman, man and woman, powerful and powerless, young and old, lucky and unlucky, those with and those without. The powerful on their lofty perches became subjects, and they deemed the vulnerable to be objects.

They stashed food and kept it for themselves, for by the logic of The Great Forgetting, their lives, desires and pleasures were more precious than those of others.

This is when Nature became confused, for Her Way is always to make things fair and even. She sends water to fill empty dams, high-pressure winds to low-pressure areas, hot air upwards to push cold air earthwards. The universe has always dispatched replacements wherever there are vacuums, to create stability when there is imbalance. Nature didn't count on the hoarders who refused to share.

Humans, as it turns out, have not been good students of Nature.

Soon they ignored the fact that everything they possessed, all they had accumulated and turned into commodities, were gifts from Nature.

The Great Forgetting led to a slew of wicked troubles, too many to count.

The problem in the world is not that there is a lack of food. There is enough.

It is not that there is a shortage of love or joy or wealth to go round. There is enough.

The problem is not that there are no solutions or miracles. They all exist aplenty.

To fix the world, humans simply need to remember their place in it.

This story is about a small person and a whale who remembered to remember.

Chapter 1

In a year buried by history, many many centuries before you were born, in a hamlet called Vilingraz, a boy crept through the shadows of the cobbled streets and headed for the ocean beyond the forest. He was accompanied by a Spanish scrub goat called Isabel, around whose neck an old fishing rope was tied so that the two might not be separated. In the pocket of his pants, a ribboned note was tucked.

The child's name was Teodoro Beneviste. He had one eye on the left that could see, and an empty eye socket on the right that he kept covered with a small patch of cloth, for it is a lamentable fact that people in possession of two eyes do not appreciate gazing upon those with one, or – even less forgivably – none.

His eye had been lost in a dreadful accident I am sure you are keen to hear about. But you will have to wait for that part of the story.

At the moment our tale begins, it was already late afternoon, and the shadows were elongating to graze each chimney, fence and wall with their long grey fingers. Were it a usual day, Teodoro might have slowed down to watch the buildings turn tea-stained as the sun sank, but this was not a usual day. We might even go so far as to say that these were not usual times. It is also true that Teodoro had not had a usual life, but up to this point, he did not know this much about himself.

His older sister, Sancia, had given him the clearest of instructions, even though she did so in a feverish sweat, with such a tremble in her hands and a voice so hoarse, it had scared the lad cold.

'Head through the forest towards the ocean. Keep close to the river. Follow the sinking sun to the cliffs of the west.'

It was enough that Sancia was sending him beyond the front door of their tiny home. That alone was a risky mission. At the mention of the forest, the ocean and the cliffs of the west, Teodoro's eye grew wide. Both he and Sancia knew this was an act of unimaginable rebellion, not to mention danger.

'There, you will find Malakha – give Her this note. Hand it to Her yourself. It is not for your eye. Promise me you will not read it.'

Shivering, Sancia pressed a fastened epistle into Teodoro's hands and handed him a hempen shoulder bag, known in these times as a scrip.

'All you need is here,' she said. 'Don't lose the letter.'

Teodoro quivered with a tremble he barely understood. Though he had nodded at Sancia's every instruction, every part of him wanted to shake no no no. Had there been a moment to pause, he might have; but, alas, there was no time. As I mentioned, these were the most extraordinarily unusual circumstances.

'It is a matter of life and death. Go, my Teo.' These words were no more than a whisper before Sancia sank backwards onto the bed and shut her eyes in a shudder.

A million questions flooded Teodoro's head and dammed themselves at his mouth. How could he turn and shut the door and leave Sancia behind? His sister – frightened by the full moon, the clatter of wheels on the cobblestones, the winds that swept through the village, the shriek of eagles, even sometimes her own heartbeat – needed him now more than ever. Who would hold her hand and stroke her back and tell her, 'There is nothing to fear,' if Teodoro were not there?

Never mind that he had never been so far from home. And all alone ... no, not alone. Isabel would go with him – goats, especially of the scrub kind, are surefooted and the shrewdest of animals. They are possessed of extraordinary eyesight, with no frontal blind spot and an uncanny discernment for edible flora and fungi. Besides her usefulness, her warm-blooded camaraderie would be a comfort on such a risky voyage. But then, the cliffs of the west were a realm beyond both their imaginations and experience; further, such a venture might endanger the goat's life, and Isabel had not consented to such jeopardy. She trusted Teodoro blindly. How could he commission such generosity from his horned and yellow-eyed donor? Still, without Isabel, Teodoro's courage could easily puncture. She was indispensable to his journey. He would ask her forgiveness upon their safe return.

Sancia was sending him – could it be so? – to Malakha. In his short life, he'd heard plenty of more than slightly dreadful whisperings of Her. That She was half-demon, half-human. That She lived in the depths of the ocean and called in the tides and the worst of storms, Gota Fría, that wrought havoc. She was said to howl at the moon and sink ships. It was a rumour, now accepted as fact, that it must have been She who had set the curse upon the fishing town of Dazic by poisoning a haul of silver fish, for the fishermen returning to port from a stormy catch had succumbed to the pox first of all. From there, it had spread through the forest to all the neighbouring hamlets, including Vilingraz, now enthralled in its snare.

So it was with barely contained trepidation that Teodoro, with his goat, set off in a grey cape – the delights of colourful garments were far beyond the reach of a poor family like his – to deliver this missive, his hempen scrip around his shoulder and a lantern lighting his way through the oncoming night.

It was a matter of life and death, and Teodoro knew whose life depended on it.

Sancia – it grieves me to impart – was gravely ill with a high fever. If she received no medicine, urgently … no, Teodoro wouldn't think such darknesses.

They had already tried all the ways two young people might devise to get even a few small drops of anti-pox tincture. Those lucky enough to have come into its possession were said to have sold their family's treasures, heirlooms, donkeys, horses and weapons to secure a few drops, and they would not part with it, not for any price, not for any begging nor for any bartering.

The time in which this story happens was deep into The Great Forgetting and the world was tilted in a way that made life for people like Teodoro and his sister – there is no other word for it – terrible. To be poor is to suffer gruesome injustices for which there seem to be no remedies, just the endless rumbles of starvation and cold and dreams of fullness and warmth in the small snatches of sleep one might grasp between hungers. In the days we are talking of, as you will by now have gathered, there was a shortage of many goodnesses, including medication – most especially for those to whom life had assigned abject poverty.

Fear and disease, however, were abundant; they festered around every corner. A strange and disastrous pandemic had been raging for many months now, and people – mothers, fathers and small children – were, I am sorry to impart, dying one after another. Shems Halevi, whose job it was to dig graves, could barely keep up with the demand. Without him, the corpses would have piled up on the streets, luring wild animals from the forest into the village square, in which once life had been a festivity of sharing and celebration.

Each day poor Shems would return home to his small ramshackle enclosure at the rim of the forest, drenched with perspiration and exertion. There he would unwind the many scarves he had tied around his mouth and nose to protect himself from the pox, remove two pairs of gloves from his hands and hunch into a broth of wild fungi prepared by Rodrigo, his son, who stuttered when he spoke.

Rodrigo would often accompany his father to help lift the deceased onto the death wagon. In this way, his young limbs grew strong while his heart grew old too early for a boy of thirteen. Once the graves had been dug and the bodies laid to rest, he would slip off into the woods to soak in the breathing womb of the forest. In this abditory of foliage, he foraged for the nightly soup, understanding that at the end of a cruel day a father who had been burying the dead might need an elixir to wash away the devastations of his labour. Sometimes he would lose time and spend days following the ribboned stream all the way down to where the great ocean beckoned and the soil became sandy. He knew the plants that grew in the shelves along the swamp, the ones called pigface, and that the sea beans sprouting on the edge of saltmarshes made tasty soup. He noted the red-flowering sedums tucked away in the embankments, the lobster mushrooms and wild roses, fiddleheads, chickweed and cattails, the ones the birds and insects ate.

He watched and remembered everything he'd seen, all the while turning words around in his head, stroking the manes of their vowels and patting the flanks of their consonants. In this way, he composed poems – not for a living, for these did not bring home a meal, but for what we might call a dreaming, which he knew was part of what made living something you kept on wanting to do.

At night he tried to soothe his father's torment with his poems, but the words that swarmed in his mind came out of his mouth too slowly, as if tripping over their own letters. In his own head, he never stumbled on phrases, nor did battle with a sibilant. His voice was unbroken – until he tried to talk. Then, as if stones and rocks and boulders had been placed in his path, he floundered and staggered, fumbled and tripped.

Rodrigo felt everything, but said little.

He and Teodoro were the best of friends. Rodrigo was one of the few who knew Teodoro's secret – that, despite appearances, Teodoro was a girl, not a boy, whose true name was Dorotea. But if anyone understood the need to shield a mystery and guard what is holy, without ever having been so instructed, it was Rodrigo.

In dreadful times, friends such as this bestow fortune, no matter how wretched one's conditions or ocular deficiencies.

If you are wondering about the motives for such elaborate subterfuge, you will have to keep reading. Now is hardly the time to disclose them.

In the meantime, let us call her Teo, like Rodrigo, for now we know her secret too.

Chapter 2

Teo wasn't especially daring. She was other things: quick and clever and brimming with curiosity that coursed through her like a silent river. The rumblings inside her were wild and endless. From what source did the sun draw its warmth? What was snow made out of? How did bears know to hide when the seasons changed and survive hunger and thirst through the long winters? Why couldn't humans do the same when food was scarce? If she had double the eyes, would she be able to see double the stars? How did it happen that her hair was the colour of copper, when Sancia's was raven-black? Did her sister's grey eyes take after those of their mother, of whom Teo could not conjure even a scrap of memory? Were her dreams of the sea because those waters held her never-coming-home mama?

Admittedly Teo was less nimble than she might have been, for having one eye almost halved what she could perceive. Now, while a blind spot is common in all sighted creatures, based on the whereabouts of their peepers, some – such as the octopus, dragonfly, chameleon and the humble goat – possess vision that renders the world a far greater visual extravaganza than those of us with a pair of frontal orbs could ever imagine. How Teo, in her thirst and curiosity, would have prized this knowledge; alas, she would never know. She knew only to adjust the angle of her head and watch her step more carefully than you or I might, presuming we have never had to lose something as irreplaceable as an eyeball.

But see, it did not matter to her that she had only one eye. She had only one sister, and for the sake of this precious circumstance she wasted no moment mired in misgiving. She gripped the note tight in her fist and shoved all the daunting tales she'd ever overheard about Malakha and the ravenous ocean and its voracious waves to the furthest corners of her thinking. With the image of her sister's burning face and the terror in her two hooded eyes driving her, Teo headed straight through the town, skirting the sides of buildings, keeping her inhibited gaze low so as not to meet the misery in her path. It took mettle to scuttle past stumblers, human castaways no-one would help, tossed from their homes, abandoned to their fate. But, if ever selfishness could be forgiven, surely it was now. She could not be distracted. She moved like this until the commotions and consternations of the entire hamlet were behind her.

There is a time for questions and a time for answers. In between, there is a time for action.

When that time comes, you will know it, as Teo knows it now.

Then, perhaps, every unanswered question heaving in your chest might quieten momentarily, as they did for Teo, even the ones about how precisely it had come to pass that their dear mama had been drowned by the ocean; and whether her eyes had held flecks of storm-bringing sky; and what manner of sillinesses had made her jingle with laughter; and how precisely the sound of her voice might have rung in Teo's ear. These speculations stridulated silently through Teo, each a plectrum on the strings of her wonder. This loss had left her with as many curiosities as aches. At times it seemed as if the years had erased her mother completely, long before memory had found its shaky legs and stood on its own feet like a newborn goat.

But there is no time nor reason to feel sorry for Teo.

To begin with, where there is an imbalance, Nature always sends compensations. So while Teo wasn't the best see-er in the world, she had more than excellent hearing. She could detect murmurs from across the street and make out the squeaks of mice in the fields, nibbling on corn. She knew when the season was about to change from one to the next because the vibration of ice melting on the river shuddered through her veins.

And though she had never seen it with her own eye, for it lay beyond the dark emerald tassel of the forest, she could taste and hear the ocean, especially when it was quiet and the clear moon rose like a cold sun in the inky sky. The smell of salt in the air stirred her hunger, with greater pangs than the scent of freshly baked bread when the breeze carried it from behind the high walls of the citadel into the slum where she lived. In the days we are speaking of, by the time bread reached the poor it was as old and hard as leather. This, I assure you, was a luxury, for it could just as easily be mouldy and crawling with maggots, discards from the kitchens of the affluent.

Her yearning for those faraway waters remained her secret, for how could she speak of it when it was the sea that had left her and Sancia without a mother, and made her beloved papa a widower? Still, the ocean called to her and many nights she imagined it in her sleep, in her keeps-coming-back dream, the one she could only ever share with Rodrigo.

Once, Merdocai Beneviste had been a talented fisherman in the seaside town of Dazic, one they called the Bream

Whisperer. But no more. He could not bear to be reminded of the slaughtering waves that had clear lapped his wife, Gracia de Luna, off the rocks where she had been chiselling oysters. By the time villagers had been called and thrown ropes into the foaming brine, it was too late. She had been gulped whole and disappeared beneath the lathering swirls. Her body was never found – not even a rag from her dress or headscarf – no matter how many days he took his boat out to search and scour the sequined skin of the sea. All that she'd left behind, wedged between two rocks, was her two-tined fork, the one Merdocai had wooed her with.

He had put away his fishing ropes and nets and left his fishing boat to rot. Without looking back, he had packed his few belongings and relocated his family to Vilingraz, way beyond the rise of the forest, so he did not have to lay his eyes upon the waters of the ocean each day. To him, it was nothing but a graveyard.

So you see, Merdocai would not have given his blessing for his youngest child to undertake such a journey. He would – to be forthright – have forbidden it. The sea had taken his Gracia, but it would touch no others of his family. What, was a new wife just to sprout like a forest mushroom overnight? Who could replace her? She had been a majestic creation, like a Pyrenean oak or a sea otter, upon whom so much life depends. In one sickening moment, she'd been sunk without a trace so that he couldn't even honour her with a proper burial. There were as many griefs inside him as there are concentric rings in the trunk of an ancient tree. He was a man stratified with sadness, a matryoshka doll of stacked sorrows.

Thus, he forbade his children from straying beyond the forest, setting foot on the sand or permitting the sea to touch their toes. The ocean was the enemy. *Never go near it.* They were to steer clear of ever eating a fish or a sea creature ever again, for who knew if it had nibbled on the flesh of their own mother? His daughters had abided by these injunctions borne from sorrow, as if to defy them would be to desecrate the holy memory of their mother, may her dear soul rest in salt.

You must be wondering where Merdocai was when Sancia pressed the note into Teo's hand and all but shooed her out the door despite her fevered delirium. A few days before our story begins, the Marquis, appointed by King Ferdinand the Innocent (an illuminating exemplar of irony) had issued a proclamation that travelled from behind the great walls of the citadel where the moneyed noble class lived far from the squalor of the poor. The news was announced in pamphlets left at the front of every barred door:

WILL YOU BE A HERO
TO END THE POX?

On the back was printed:

SCIENTIFIK Experiments by Doctors
ONE HUNDRED PER CENT Safe.
SUBMIT YOUR MORTAL BODY
For The Greater Good Before it is
TOO LATE.
REWARD: The Marquis' GRATITUDE
& 1 Hen + 1 Sack of Royal Wheat
(no Weevils)

The poor flung their doors open and grabbed the flyers. The few who could read understood the offer; those who couldn't called to their neighbours, begging the literate amongst them to share the news. But in times of scarcity, people clutch information as if it were stomach-filling rations. Fragments spilled onto the cobble streets, drifted under doors, trickled through cracks in floorboards and windows, mumbled and repeated and passed from mouth to ear and ear to mouth. The message was elaborated, invented, mangled and twisted.

The pox will end The Greater Good.

Scientifik experiments on one hundred weevils.

It is too late to become a hero.

Merdocai Beneviste, who since relinquishing the life of a fisherman had learned the art of wheel-fixing, stood and held the pamphlet of many long moments, his hat in his other hand

The Greater Good. Who could ask for more? What sort of man didn't wish to become a *hero*, roused to action for the benefit of others in times of hopeless inertia?

These words ignited something inside him. They glowed, radiant and vivid, even as the terror of every man, woman and child clattered behind every door. Should he, or shouldn't he? Yes, of course he should. No, what on earth was he thinking, when he had two children to take care of? He landed where he always did, on the crest of this one enduring thought: *What would Gracia de Luna say?*

She would have reminded him that the Marquis could not keep a promise if it were tied to him like a donkey. Not if he were manacled to it and the key thrown into the ocean. Not if it grew out of his squat little body like a second head. Not if he swallowed it whole – he'd shit it out before sundown. When honour was being handed out by the Almighty Creator, the Marquis must have been on a hunt for yet another poor beast to hang in his chamber – for surely it was only the beheaded who could abide to gaze upon him? Oh, Gracia de Luna could make one chuckle. Once she took hold of a thought, she'd toss it higher and higher into the branches of hilarity until

Merdocai expelled a full-bellied laugh, no matter his worries or troubles. She had enlarged everything she ever touched, the way the light of day reveals the landscape hidden by night.

Merdocai counted on his eight fingers the number of times the Marquis had vowed an end to this shortage and that outage, a fixing of one calamity and the restoration of another collapse. He flaunted fine speeches, but as soon as a promise left his mouth, his pledges dropped from his memory like coins through a hole in a pocket. *Like water in a leaky bucket. Goat droppings after a feed*, Merdocai imagined his once-upon-a wife uttering.

Despite the temptation of the Marquis' offering, Merdocai faltered on one phrase:

ONE HUNDRED PER CENT.

Oh, Merdocai knew a falsehood when he heard it. The only way to hear the truth was to place one palm on the heart and one on the belly, close down the eyes and repeat the words over and over. Gracia de Luna had taught him this.

Merdocai replaced his hat on his head and walked briskly home through the shortening light, resolved, yes, resolved that this was a cruel hoax, a devious ploy by a shrewd politician who did not care at all for the lives of the poor, even as the words *Greater Good*, *hero* and *reward* glimmered like faint torches inside him.

But the next morning, when he woke to find Sancia burning with fever, he made up his mind in an instant.

'If there is even a ONE PER CENT chance of finding a cure, I will go,' he declared to his girls.

Teo had pleaded, 'But, Papa, what if these medicines make you grow horns? Or turn your hands into hooves? Or render you blind? What if they are poisonous?'

'But what if they are miraculous, my sweetling?'

These words emerged as if Gracia herself were speaking through him. She had talked as easily of miracles as of meals: what one wished was as likely to eventuate as what one shucked. She was a dream-reaper, diviner of weather patterns and the future, while Merdocai could only read the spirit of the times.

When the rains are slow to arrive and the crops collapse in the fields, and every man, woman and child is struck out of their wits with hunger and desperation, and then – oh, calamity upon calamity – a pox hails down like a noxious downpour, a ruler will find someone to blame. It is, after all, human nature to seek illogical answers to scientific questions. It grieves me to impart that many a woman and girl in the town had been accused of witchcraft and tortured or done away with in the name of The Greater Good. From the moment Teo came into his world, Merdocai feared that her strange and marvellous difference, single eye and astonishing otherworldly arrival would make her a target for such indictments.

The simple fact of girlhood alone was a treacherous circumstance in such a calamitous and blame-hurtling age. So Teo's father had devised a plan; perhaps, in hindsight, not the most cunning, but the sodden keening of grief has been known to afflict the pattern of a man's judgment. It is self-evident that all children belong to the world in both boyish and girlish ways, until a certain time of life presses a choice, like a fork in the woods going this way and that. For the time being, Merdocai determined it was safer for Teo to be a boy. To this end, he kept her hair short. He dressed her in boy's clothes. He gave her boyish tasks. But it was becoming trickier with every passing spring to hold the secret down. Merdocai dreaded that he would not be able to shield her much longer. And now, to protect Sancia, he would gamble on this tiny chance.

'No, Papa, do not sacrifice yourself,' Sancia sobbed from her bed.

'Better I should offer myself than wait for this disease to take either of you,' he replied. 'At least with an egg-laying hen and a sack of wheat, I can rest knowing you will be taken care of … even in the event …' Merdocai did not end a sentence that needed no finishing.

The thin porridge in their bowls grew colder as the little family contemplated the desolation that this stunted sentence implied.

When danger comes, some people will trample everyone and everything in their path to get themselves to safety. Others will put their hands up to wade through the darkness first, even as it deepens, offering themselves as prey to whatever perils are lying in wait so that they might build safe passage for those behind them. This is how the world is truly and naturally divided: into some and others. By example, Merdocai showed his type. Without imposing on his children a single utterance or instruction, he carved out a path forward that they would always follow without doubting it was the right one, even as others around them flocked in the opposite direction.

Chapter 3

In his chamber in the high streets of the citadel that governed the hamlet of Vilingraz, the Marquis, Don Lazaro de Abismo held a lifeless mouse by its tail. He dangled it in front of his albino goshawk, Dante.

The bird lowered his head and turned his beak to the side. Something was hideously amiss. The Marquis clenched his jaw as he dropped the mouse to the floor and turned away from the creature deteriorating before his eyes.

'I'll just leave it here, in case you change your mind.'

It would not do to let Dante see his distress. Why, the Marquis himself had been dispossessed of an appetite the past months, so much so that he'd cinched his belt a notch tighter to hold up his gold-embossed maroon pantaloons. It was impossible to tell whether his prized raptor was simply a mirror, mimicking his own mounting panic at the havoc and mayhem the pox had unleashed, all under his governance. An epidemic scouring through the slums, disposing of the weak and useless, was to be hailed, ¡Hurra! and so forth. But when it breached frontiers with noxious indiscrimination and began picking off the strong and ennobled, halting trades and bringing the hamlet to its knees, *no servirá*! He had to control, contain and reverse it all – and swiftly.

He swivelled slowly back and lowered the tone of his voice.

'I do understand,' he crooned, stroking Dante's chest. 'You want it alive so you can kill it yourself. Soon, I shall take you out into the fields for a rabbit. Or a field mouse? Would you fancy that, a squirming vole whose heart you can pluck out with your beak? I shall end this pox, have no doubt, and we shall be free to roam again.'

From the corner of his eye, the Marquis glimpsed a scuttling across the marbled floor. He paused as the cockroach approached, skittish with plans.

Lifting his one strong leg, he slammed it down, but the bug had scurried to safety long before the heeled boot landed. His gammy leg knotted in a cramp, discharging a ventriloquy of curses from the Marquis' pursed lips. Please note, the word 'gammy' would have been forbidden by the Marquis as a description of his weakened limb; his authority, however, does not extend to the narration of our story. His leg had been this way since his difficult birth. He had almost died, but had eventually come out not head but feet first. Such a birth might have marked him as a stand-out, one-less-ordinary, a man destined for greatness, for hadn't he entered the world by 'landing on his feet'? Instead, the attending midwife had yanked him by his left leg to release him from his mother's womb, and had broken it in the process, leaving him somewhat hobbled. But nature had not intended for him to be crippled. He was an accident misfortune had made. Perfection ruined by recklessness.

The careless midwife had paid the price – he had seen to it. But she had ruined him forever. He was never free from it, the plague of outrageous pity in the eyes of his inferiors. Even so. Consider how he had overcome the shackles of his beginnings. Apprise, if you will, how he had risen in the ranks to be one of the most powerful people in the land. A marquis, no less. Wasn't he a breathing model of how the world was divided into winners and losers? Triumph was not a result of trying but inherent to the design, as was its opposite, feeble-mindedness. Superiority was innate: a matter of science, not human will.

The mouse on the floor began to ooze its entrails. With a queasy stomach the Marquis summoned his subordinate. 'Torrero! *Avance!*'

The sound of his own voice hollering to underlings always revived him. Was there anything more uplifting to the spirit than dominion over minions? To hold the fates of others in the words one uttered, to inspire trepidation and awe simply by barking and watching chumps jump, was a heady rush.

Graviel Torrero presented himself with a salute, donning his ill-fitting headgear. He had a remarkably large cranium in proportion with the rest of his dimensions, and helmets were simply not manufactured with such girth in mind.

The Marquis could not help but marvel at the sheer perplexing heft of the man in front of him. Why, his fingers were as thick as carrots, his forearms as wide as branches of an elm. Had he not been so savagely stunted at birth surely he too would have grown into a titan. No-one speaks of the violation of a man's esteem when he feels robbed of the prospects of stature and his birthright to physical eminence.

'Clean up this mess.' He gestured.

Graviel hesitated. Was this not the goshawk's dinner? He had only just been ordered to find and trap a mouse in the imperial barns. He could still feel it quivering under his hand as he drowned it in a bucket of water.

'Bring me a live one!'

Graviel nodded, bent down with great effort and lifted the mouse by the scruff of its tiny neck. Its eyes were glazed with the hereafter.

'What is the news of the miserable riff-raff? How many have offered themselves for the experiment?' the Marquis asked.

Graviel paused. 'One.'

The Marquis curled his lips. 'Is that helmet too tight?'

'It pinches. A little,' Graviel managed.

'It stunts your brain, Torrero.' The Marquis' voice was icy. 'What slips your mind?'

Graviel blinked. What had he forgotten? He was generally adept at following orders. His thoughts were blank.

'What am I? To you?'

Ah. Graviel exhaled. 'Muy Ilustre Señor Marqués,' he corrected.

'Begin afresh.'

Afresh, Graviel noted. 'There is but one, Muy Ilustre Señor Marqués, Don Lazaro de Abismo.'

The Marquis huffed. 'A singleton? What is wrong with these wastelings? What more could they hope for in their lowly doomed lives? A chicken, wheat free of weevils. What prevents them from trampling each other to submit themselves? What madness has possessed them?'

Before he could think about whether he really wanted to say what was perched on his tongue, a small, 'Perhaps ...' slipped out from under Graviel Torrero's moustache. This, he instantly regretted.

The corners of the Marquis' lips lifted, exposing his teeth. It was a morphological shift of his mouth involving up to forty-three facial muscles. In any other circumstance, this might have been conceived as a smile and an invitation to reciprocate with one's own beamish gesture. But Graviel Torrero had learned to perceive these expressions as optical illusions, reversing his notions of what things meant into mistaken misconceptions.

'Elaborate,' the Marquis encouraged, and then, under his breath but not so silently that it went unheard, '*bobo grande.*'

Graviel could not be certain of the precise meaning of the four-syllabled word, though '*bobo grande*' he'd heard aplenty, an insult to remind the foolish that they were so. Still, he could place things in their right order and calculate by deduction. 'Elaborate' must here mean 'go on', and apart from wishing the Marquis would simply say what he meant, he also wished he was sitting at home by the fire, with his wife, Taresa, and their newborn daughter, Beatris. Beatris, Beatris, Beatris. Was there a more beautiful sound in the world than that? No, there was not; of this he was certain. He desired with all his inclinations not to be standing in a tight-fitting uniform with a scarcely tolerable pain in his lower back, in front of the Marquis who was awaiting his answer. Graviel lamented his blunt wit, which did not enable him to conjure up some excuse or lie on the spot. All he could think was to dribble out the truth.

'Perhaps … because the medicine is still so …'

The Marquis twirled his facial hair. Of his many talents, none was so lethal as that for siphoning the confidence it took for a man to utter a single word, even from those who towered over him, like Graviel Torrero.

'Primitive …?' Graviel all but murmured, surprising even himself, for life presents even the *bobos* amongst us with opportunities to proffer the occasional three-syllabled word.

The Marquis paused. 'Primitive. Derived from ancient Latin of course, you know that. *Primus*, "first", *primitivus*, "the first of its kind". So you appreciate there can be no progress without trial and error?'

Graviel heard a faint voice in his head telling him not to tumble into utterance, but the message arrived too late for his mouth. 'I meant … uncertain.' He paused. 'Muy Ilustre Señor Marqués.'

Marquis Lazaro de Abismo plonked down in his lavish chair, adorned with his coat of arms, using as much heaviness as his smallness could muster. 'Uncertainty is the key to advancement, yes?'

Graviel was himself uncertain, but he nodded anyway.

'All that is certain is that the poor are dispensable. Vermin, like that mouse.' He gestured to the rodent dangling from Graviel's enormous fingers. 'What greater fate could await a rat than to be experimented on for the sake of prospering its superiors?' The Marquis waited. 'Well?'

Graviel bobbed more than nodded his large head. The mouse in his hand bobbled backwards and forwards like a pendulum.

The Marquis narrowed his eyes. 'But you are preoccupied.'

Graviel swallowed.

'How do they fare? The wife and newborn? Do report.'

Words gripped Graviel's lips, recoiling, for it is a punishment to speak of sacred things in places that do not honour their sanctity.

'Healthy, *gracias*, Muy Ilustre Señor Marqués.'

'What more could a man ask?' The Marquis smiled coldly.

Graviel shrugged.

'To keep them that way, surely?'

'*Sí*, to keep them that way. Muy Ilustre Señor Marqués.'

'So you agree then. We need Subject Matters for the experiment, and so far our efforts have come to almost nothing. We have but one. What use is one? Pah!'

Graviel found himself nodding. It seemed to be all he could muster.

'What did your father teach you about fishing?'

Graviel winced. Any titbit of personal knowledge the Marquis seized turned in his delicate hands into an instrument of excruciation. Graviel's father had been a merchant. He'd spent his days on ships. Best of all, he knew birds. They had drawn his esteem and curiosity in a way his own offspring never could. Never once had his father taken him fishing.

The Marquis became impatient. 'What did he teach you about bringing in a catch?'

Graviel thought hard. A net. A boat. A hook. Which was the correct answer?

'A lure,' the Marquis answered his own question. 'So how shall we entice these *idiotas indigentes*?' He closed his eyes as if conjuring a vision.

The Marquis understood the way words cast spells. They could be turned a degree, curated, repeated in a certain order, and by this tinkering, could elicit unlikely associations. A story was like dough that could be twisted into any shape. All it took was a kernel of truth wrapped in a muslin of lies, fed to the feckless. Why, all one needed was to forbid people to think of an alabaster salamander, and in that moment, they could not help but conjure up the very prohibited preposterousness. The human mind was a mire, and the Marquis had a bent for aiding its entanglements.

'This is a rare – no – a once-in-a-lifetime opportunity … for …' He paused. Opportunity? That was too many syllables … chance was punchier. 'This is the Chance of a Lifetime … for … for Redemption. Yes, a biblical word will do it. To be on the … The Right Side of History. A Pioneer. A Man Less Ordinary. To Rise Above Your Lowly Lot in Life.' The Marquis paused. As he spoke again, he trotted back and forth, enamoured of his own plans. 'Renew our publicity and include all this … bait. Lay it on thick, double, triple thick … but where is your quill, your parchment, Torrero? Would you have me repeat all this just for your sake? Because you are half asleep on your feet?'

Graviel turned and exited the chamber to dispose of the mouse and retrieve the tools of transcription, even as they summoned the most painful of his childhood memories. Scribing had never come easily to him. In fact, one of his fingers was still bent where a schoolmaster had broken it with a rod for his poor penmanship. Once back in the presence of the Marquis, Graviel dipped the quill in the ink, his large fingers trembling, then knelt and began painstakingly to note down the Marquis' commands.

Slowly, letter by letter, he penned the only word he could recall from the Marquis's instructions: *FEET*.

The Marquis waited. 'Well, do you have it all down?'

Graviel couldn't remember anything else. But he continued to scribble *BEATRIS*, just as the ink ran out.

'*Sí*, I have it all down. Muy Ilustre Señor Marqués.'

'Distribute the pamphlets throughout the slums. Place them inside bags of grain – we have a few moth-ridden ones that are no use – and leave them in the town square. That will bring them out like pests from every corner.'

At this, Graviel panicked. What else had the Marquis said besides *feet*? He thought he'd heard the word *bait* somewhere in there. In truth, he had been preoccupied thinking of the way his baby daughter had grabbed hold of his finger that morning and squeezed it. There was nothing he would not do to keep her safe. This conviction sat right beside his unease that the pox was out there, haunting the hamlet. Apart from keeping her locked away from the world, he could not guarantee to protect her from it. What if it found its way in? Under the floorboards, on the winds, down the chimneys? One day you were well, the next you were flattened with fevers and chills, your lips were blue, your skin on fire. By day three, you were coughing. By day six, you were dead.

And with the word *dead* circling in his head, he clicked his heels and saluted the Marquis. He turned and left, bewildered at how some men were destined to become barkers, and he, of all fates, had ended up a jumper.

Chapter 4

At the time this chapter begins, Teo has left the stricken outskirts far behind her and the forest is not far ahead. She could still remember the marketplaces of holding, smelling, singing and dancing, and every part of her missed it. In just one year, the village had become a cauldron of panic. There had once been a time when it was not like this. Now people were afraid to touch and be touched; to look each other full in the face, issue invitations and barter salt for honey, flour for a dried cod. Doors had become barriers, rather than thresholds of hospitality.

Though she felt the nostalgia personally and keenly, in all the longing she withheld for things to return to how they had been, it could not go unnoticed that everyone and everything had been distorted by these restraints. Nothing had prepared people who needed one another for such bereavements.

As the familiarity of what she had always called home receded, a shadow passed over her that had nothing to do with the afternoon light. It was unlike the feeling of being watched, which moved inside her at every moment. This is how she acquired her habit of turning time and time again, to look over her shoulder – and not on account of her single eye. How might she describe this new sensation to Rodrigo? It was as though she was making a final passage through these places. No, that was not quite right – she did not doubt she would pass this way again, but it would not be with the same eye. Sometimes, when the future beckons, what we are leaving is not places, but the selves we are, behind.

How had she not heard it before? The moaning of the hamlet behind her, like a grieving choir.

Then Rodrigo's answer came back to her, when once she inquired how his father, Shems, could stand the endless reek of dead bodies. It had taken Rodrigo some time to answer, due both to his sensibility and his stutter. For the sake of haste – for time is now of the essence – this is what he said:

'A bad smell becomes just a smell over time. Like a mournful child without a mother, becomes just a child. We change to fit wherever we are.'

Teo knew he was speaking for himself as well as her. In the village, her ears had become accustomed to grief. You had to go far away so you could see and hear things as they truly are.

Now, as she stood with her goat on a rope at the lip of the forest, she looked up at the clouds. Something was gathering in the skies. It was still a way off, but she could sense it coming.

'Isabel, we have not told Rodrigo where we are going. However, will he know where we are? Will he worry?'

But what was Teo to do now? She was in the midst of the life-or-death-ness of a task on which everything turned.

Sancia's life.

Teo's too. For what would it mean to live without the warmth and lustre of the single being who made you one of the only three things that mattered in the world – a sister, a daughter, a friend?

Before the days of the pox, when people were free to rove, Teo had often trailed behind Rodrigo into the woods when an afternoon offered itself. As her chaperone, he'd led her into the laboratory of mosses, lichens and bird-brimming overhangs, where he became a different kind of Rodrigo, as if his body held many sorts of him.

Trees put Rodrigo at ease. In the forest, he unruffled. His shoulders relaxed. When it was just them-two, pillared by the elms and birches, the pines and poplars, underscored by silvery thread, tamarisk moss and spiny gorse – would you believe? – he lost the stutter that fractured his words. It was a happening both startling and undeniable. Was it sparked by the slackening of his trapezius, unclenching the four muscles of his tongue in anatomical cahoots, smoothing the staccato of his speech into legato? Or perhaps disfluency became peripheral, with only Teo and maritime pines as his audience, so that the pocket of his brain tasked with speech forgot its own inhibition?

We cannot know, so how can we ever say? It was a phenomenon upon which Teo never remarked, as if to look at it straight on might scare it away. So neither of them ever spoke of this curiosity, though she wondered about all the enigmas it held.

The woods were a kingdom of bracken fern, with its large triangular fronds, and stag, longhorn and jewel beetles in the underbrush. It was home to the shrill cat-like calls of the pine martens and the knot of toads at the edge of the river; the songs of woodpeckers, treecreepers and firecrests rang in their ears. Wandering a few paces behind her friend, who halted every so often to ensure the smoothness of her path, Teo had learned to forage. Rodrigo had taught her where to look for the boletes, chanterelles and parasol mushrooms, the blueberries and strawberries, nettles, dandelions and plantain. You could enter the forest empty-handed and leave with your scrip overflowing. Here one could be true to one's own spontaneity and be compensated at every turn by the casual offerings of this yielding realm.

But since the pox, such pilgrimages of companionship were forbidden. The two pined for one another in all the unspoken ways friends do. Despite decrees to keep people distanced, unless their labour was an 'essential service', at the end of an ordinary day Rodrigo would often take the long way home and pass by Teo's front door to drop off a bundle of scavenged plants and herbs, with a small knock-knock.

Then, through the keyhole, they would converse.

'What did you find today?' Teo would ask. 'Tell me all the colours and sounds of the forest, please. Skip no details. I want to smell and taste them all on my tongue.'

'A b-baby f-f-fox, c-c-c-opper as the m-m-mor-n-ning l-l-light, b-b-bl-lack eyes l-lik-k-e sh-shining coal.'

'Oh, oh, oh.' Teo sighed as she closed her eye and summoned the sight into her inner seeing.

'W-w-wild b-black-ber-r-r-ries, swe … s-sweet and b-b-lack-k as a c-cr-crow's sh-sh-shadow.'

'Rodrigo, you know they are my favourites.'

Though she could not see through the wooden door, she knew that on the other side the shy lilt of his lips would be reaching for his cheeks. Teo was adept in dimpling Rodrigo with delight, sometimes discomposing him into laughter.

Rodrigo and Shems dwelt at the edge of the forest, some distance from Vilingraz. They had been forced to leave their home in the centre of the village by their neighbours, who did not want a man who touched the contaminated deceased living in their midst. They wished only that their dead be disposed of, while absconding their presence, lest the lifeless grab them and pull them down into the grave with them. They'd leave bodies on the street and when Shems drove by with his cart and horse, they'd sometimes toss a few *dineros* through the window or door for his efforts. These dinged as they landed on the cobblestones, clinking of hypocrisy, which, if we can bear the truth, is a tendency hidden in every one of us, coaxed to the fore by a particular, desolate pattern of circumstances.

Shems collected these pennies dolefully, for he had a son to feed.

Not only did he undertake the exertions involving shovels and earth and interment to dispose of dead bodies, he also tendered blessings for each life extinguished; words rose up in him as naturally as an expelled breath as he covered each body with soil.

'Rest your soul, for you worked your body to the bone.'

'May Heaven receive you with open arms.'

'You were too young to depart, fair child.'

'May your suffering be ever gone.'

There was no-one to receive these soft mumbles. The words landed gently, like snowflakes in an untraversed part of the world, where some may say there are no witnesses. But that is only if you do not also count the worms, aphids, beetles, stars and quiet motes of dust that gather like a holy congregation whenever anything dies.

Rodrigo came from a small family – just those left behind. A mother, dead of tuberculosis when her child was less than two years old. A father, frozen in mid-stride, never having imagined what could lie beyond the promise 'to love and hold' made three autumns before.

As a woodsman, Shems had just taken out a huge loan from the Marquis to start his own joinery business of building doors and windows, the carpentry of comings and goings, when his first job was to build a coffin for his wife, Josefa. What did it mean to 'start over'? He had just started out. He had consented to none of it – how could he choose a dress in which to bury Josefa? (Her handmade wedding dress or the black one for funerals? Which one? Which one? The wedding dress won.) Was Shems to lie with his small boy as he whimpered himself to sleep, when it was the child's mother who had nursed him through the night? What was he to feed a child, day in and day out?

It was like a sudden, erroneous prison sentence, an inexplicable bewildering circumstance with no fault, blame or solution. One day he was newly married with a son, the next he was a widower with a motherless child. There seemed no bridge between those versions of his life. So he stayed where he was, scrabbling in the small patch of dust in between, unable to offer Rodrigo any consolations from the valley of his own defeat before life had even given him a chance to prove what he was capable of.

In the months that followed, Shems lost all his teeth, one by one – we might surmise, from grief. He buried each one in a tooth grave beside Josefa's.

Rodrigo worked beside his father, who had never spoken much before Josefa died and who lost most of his vocabulary, or so it seemed, after she did. Rodrigo came to trust the silences. They were harbours; there was no need to fill them, but you could always pull into one for safety.

In these moments, though Shems could not speak, he could cry. At night after he put little Rodrigo to bed, Shems would sit alongside him in a chair and weep freely. It was a sound Rodrigo became familiar with, the small creaks of anguish that pulsed from the throat, in between silent sobs when darkness amplified sorrow. Once, Rodrigo crept out of bed and came to stand in front of his father, who looked up at him with a face barely recognisable to the boy. Rodrigo stood and watched. He beheld his father crying, like he might have watched a wounded animal suffer, and Shems let him. In that moment, though no words passed between them, a heritage was passed down between father and son, and though Shems had not been given the time to prove what a good man could achieve in a good life, he offered all his goodness to Rodrigo, who gathered it up: *It is okay for a man to cry.*

Rodrigo never regarded crying as a weakness, but a refuge. Tears were precious. He held onto his, like interest accruing on a modest saving, knowing someday, when they were needed, he would be able to withdraw and expend them wisely.

In the presence of tears, Rodrigo became mute, a witness, as he had always done for his father. There was so much sorrow in these times, and though he did not cry himself, when others cried, he received their tears without judgment or alarm. When you were with him, you felt somehow all right. That is because Rodrigo knew something existed on the other side of grief, and he was not afraid of it.

You could say he was someone who made you feel that one thing you need when everything feels lost: hope.

Chapter 5

We now find Teo and Isabel at the threshold of the forest. But not for long, as they are already traipsing ahead on the well-worn path, so let's keep up.

Only as they entered the woods, with its corridors of shadows and shaded secrets, did it occur to Teo that there were many questions she should have asked Sancia before she set off. But it was too late to inquire, *Exactly where am I going? And why? And what for?* The ocean, Malakha, her dear papa – where was he now? And oh, Sancia.

If you have ever had the slimy leeches of doubt crawl upon you, you too will know what a vehemence of courage it takes to squelch the terror and nonetheless proceed.

Would Teo make it back, with a cure, in time to save her sister? When would her papa return? Was there a cure for the pox, or was all forever lost?

These are many hesitations for a young person to be carrying and could, if one let them, cause a conflagration of confusion and a misery of purpose. But Teo understood only that Sancia was sick and the hours were running thin. Sometimes all you need to know is that you have no choice. It is when a heart is cleaved that the feet falter.

Without Rodrigo, it was an utterly different experience to venture into the woodlands. He knew the forest as kin and belonged to it more fully than to the peopled whereabouts of the village. He gave his own names to its paths and places – not to seize possession like a marquis, but as a courtship with the terrain. It comforted Teo to have the markers Slender Mouse-tail Moss Juncture, Spiny-gorse Grove, Waved Silk Moss Boulder and Deadwood Beech Cairn in her mouth to parse their journey. Ahead of her stood the great holm oak he called Abuela Guardiana, the Grandmother Guardian that had lived many human lifetimes encircled with her mossy petticoat of sphagnum. She too had a hollowed-out aperture like an eye emptied of its eyeball, and for this likeness, and many other affinities, Teo felt a bond with her.

'Remember, *Abuela*, I have passed by,' Teo whispered.

Beyond this ancient sentinel, the forest changed. It became thicker, darker and harder to push through. Teo took a kneeling moment to light her lantern with the flint in her scrip and muster herself before proceeding by the modest glow of her lamp. It occurred to her that she was in possession of the single source of light her family owned, save for the fire, which by this stage would have dwindled to ash. Alone, Sancia would be engulfed in darkness; at this thought, which arose in her mind as a picture, a small sob escaped Teo's mouth and made her pick up her pace.

The patter of Isabel's feet on the undergrowth crackled. Rabbits rustled invisibly. Tree frogs croaked and critters crooned. Every now and then Teo paused, as Isabel stopped, her ears gyrating to take in the yipping, skittering, twittering and rustling that came from all directions. Teo glanced over her shoulder every few paces, as if eyes were upon her. She was, of course, being watched by all the flora and fauna, both hidden and revealed, but was there some other surveying force in the ether? It felt this way as each tiny sound passed through Teo like an endless tinkling of life's symphonies. At the base of it all was a vibration that came from beyond the forest, in the direction of the *Never go near it* ocean. It whirred and clicked in her inner ear, in a pattern she almost recognised but did not understand.

Now and then, it felt like a secret call, like sometimes happens between two people who are destined to meet down the crease of time and who carry each other inside until that fated moment.

Approximately five miles from the shore of Dazic, which is a fair distance by any ambulant standards, far out at sea, a blue whale rose from the depths to the surface and gulped in oxygen. He was eighty-nine years old or thereabouts, though no human had counted his birthdays, and it took every ounce of energy left in his hulk to breach.

There would not be many more he would manage.

As he lifted the tank of his body above the skin of the sea, under which he had swum and frolicked for nearly a century, he slowed time down so he could drink in the life-giving air. With his soft eyes, he took it all in: the cirrus clouds above, the blinking horizon, the yellow-legged gulls and the sandwich terns screeching and swooping. As he thundered back down into the waves, he was complete with every encounter he'd had, from the moment he was calved by his mother in the bay and had made his way into the wondrous waters of the wide world.

It was near.

His time was coming. Soon he would be too weary to lift himself out of the water and breathe again.

Then he would drown.

His life had been rich and full. He was home to a civilisation of barnacled beings who lived on the planet of his body.

Oh, the wonders he had seen in the ocean of everythingness.

He knew that when the moment came for him to take his last breath, the weight of his body would drag him down down down into the unfathomable bottom of the dark below. Then something much bigger and more magical than even his life would happen – a consequence that would keep the world he loved nourished and prosperous for more than fifty years after his death, and feed trillions of life forms for decades to come.

Whalefall.

His own demise was already behind him, and he was far ahead of it.

He was not sad, nor sorry, nor afraid. This was the culmination of what he was here to do. An event so wondrous, generous and life-sustaining, in which every bit of plankton he'd ever sucked into his great mouth and every mouthful of krill he'd ever siphoned from the waters would now be passed on to new generations.

He was about to break into a million blessings.

It beckoned; it was so close.

Teo held tight to the rope and let Isabel lead her over carpets of pine needles as she inhaled the green of mint, juniper and eucalyptus, decaying leaves and earthy beings. Nighttime was sneaking in. As day slipped back into the pocket of time, how much further could they traverse without a high, bright moon to guide them?

All the while, she couldn't stop thinking about the keeps-coming-back dream, which came to her on many a night as she slept.

In her dream, she is always being carried away. She is wrapped in a blanket of water, and she cries for her mama. Every time she opens her mouth, she swallows saltwater. Eventually she is breathing the sea. This is how she becomes a fish. She sinks into the deep, dark ocean, until she is swimming alongside a living thing as large as a mountain. It croons to her, as if passing something on to her without words, and she is to keep its song, like one might ask a friend to hold a secret. The whole world sits inside it, like an egg about to be laid. It is the kind of love song one might sing before one departs. It is filled with the answers to all the questions she has about life, even though she doesn't understand the language.

She always wakes filled and emptied at the same time.

Teo asked everyone she knew about the dream.

Papa said, 'It's your imagination. I sometimes dream I can fly. But do I have wings?'

Sancia had frowned, all her fears scuttling into the furrow of her brow. 'It's an omen. Stay away from the ocean, Teo. And never tell anyone about your dreams. You know what happens to people who do.'

Teo knew all too well the fate of Dreamspeakers. In these long-forgotten times, it pains me to impart, trials of those accused of witchcraft were conducted by binding their limbs together and tossing them into the river. Floaters were punished with a ghastly fate, enough to gnaw your faith in human kindness to a splinter. Sinkers were pardoned as innocent, but you must see why this was no exoneration – to drown blameless is still to drown. The only dereliction of which such dreamers were guilty was being unable to swim.

Yet Teo could not help herself and had once, on a forest walk, asked Rodrigo in a brave voice.

Rodrigo, as you know, was not glib, and not only because he had a stutter. Teo's question landed on him as a green Spanish moon moth might alight upon his outstretched hand. He was silent with it, not to squeeze the knuckles of his thinking around a matter, but to draw his attention closer and closer, until part of him palpitated with the rhythm of it.

'Could it be a memory?'

'A memory? But how can I remember what never happened?'

'Maybe a buried memory? A memory before remembering began?'

'Oh, Rodrigo, you speak in riddles.' Teo had sighed. 'When does remembering begin? And who keeps the things that are forgotten?'

Rodrigo walked on in footfall of such serenity and for so long that Teo wondered if he'd left her questions behind. But Rodrigo did not forget. Just then, an ibex had stepped out from between the trees, a sighting so uncommon and unexpected that Teo covered her mouth to muffle her squeal. The ibex stood gallant and poised, appraising them both, before it bowed its head and slipped between the shadows, in all likelihood, forever.

Isabel stopped to nibble on tufts of grass, but there was no time for this lollygagging. Night was tumbling out from God's pouch, and soon the air would be too dark for furthering. Teo apologised and nudged her along.

'Papa's explanation is the right one, or is it Sancia's? No, it's Rodrigo who truly understands. But surely, Papa knows best.'

It was always Rodrigo's words that she returned to. But how could she have a memory of something she could not remember? And if Rodrigo was right, what secrets had happened to her and how would she ever learn the truth of who she was?

Chapter 6

In a dungeon in the citadel, further from daylight than even the remotest reaches of the forest, Merdocai Beneviste huddled on the icy stone floor without so much as a scratchy blanket to cover himself. His modest clothes, such as they were, had been confiscated. His head and beard had been shaved. He had stood bewildered, yielding to this accosting of his person because … because the medical trials, The Greater Good, the cure for the pox.

But where were the doctors? The researchers? Why was he being handled like a criminal? Where were the revered scientists working day and night to find a cure? No-one would address him nor answer his questions.

In moments such as these, the sudden calamity of realisation dawns. How he must have wept when he saw through the veils and the lies – in this place and moment, he was not a father, a widow, a learned man who had taught his children how to read and write. He was nothing but a lump of flesh, lowlier than even a donkey, though why asses don't deserve the utmost kindness for their uncomplaining labour is a reflection only on the shortcomings of human compassion, not on those patient hoofed mammals of the family Equidae.

Along with his beard, his humanity had been shorn. Oh, the portent of it, the simple starkness of those tufts dropping from his body only to be swept away like dirt. The inkling he had nurtured, the doubts he had carted all the way from the poorest slum up to the citadel, now weighed him down like boulders. Each of us knows in a hidden vault of the soul when we are safe and when we are in danger, but we often, with shrewd argument and circumventing logic, insist on a path that leads us into perfidy. Why we do this, it must be surmised, is another of the great unsolved mysteries of the world.

Right about now is when Merdocai Beneviste had what is known as an epiphany. But in the manner of many such enlightenments, it had come too late – in retrospect, which is often the direction wisdom travels.

In the tiny, dank quarters, without even a small window to the outdoors, he was as alone as it is humanly possible to be. There was not another mortal voice, nor another's beating pulse to match his own. Loneliness is a treachery to the spirit. Nothing is made to exist all by itself. If only we could whisper the truth into Merdocai's ears: no-one is ever alone, even if it feels that way.

Lean in with me, if you will, to look again more closely, for Merdocai is the subject of scrutiny and curiosity by a clustering of cockroaches, spiders, mice and rats. They stream in through the cracks in the stones and the slimmest apertures leading to the bowels of the earth. They skitter across the floor, encircle him, scamper across his feet; some even take their cheeky chances by nibbling him. And who can blame them? The hungers of the miniscule are just as urgent as those of the largest.

For the first days, he pounded on the heavy leaden door, pleading, calling and begging to be let out.

'My name is Merdocai Beneviste. I am a father of two. I was once a fisherman. I am a wheel-maker. I lost my wife. My children have no-one but me. I have made an error – let me go home.'

But no-one could hear his banging. In this soundless vacuum, he understood that he had fallen into the darkest depths of hell.

How could he have made such a terrible mistake?

What medical trials were these? What evil plan was in place for which he, like a foolish, naive child, had volunteered? Why had he thrown away his life with his two blessed daughters, who made him laugh and smile and anguish and hope and dream and labour each day to bring home a crust?

It is a slow-dawning shame to the one hoodwinked and misled. Why had he not listened to his heart when it said, *Never trust a man who says, 'one hundred per cent'*? How disappointed Gracia de Luna would have been to see him like this, the slave of the Marquis' chicanery. What style of a chump was he? He had failed, not only as a husband but as a father.

When a man who is composed of dignity and principle is cast into an underworld of despair, his best intentions mangled into absurdity, he will begin by blaming himself. When someone who is willing to sacrifice himself for The Greater Good is brought to his knees without knowing why or for whose benefit he is suffering, he may lose trust in himself. The phantoms of his soul will entangle him, like a bream in a fishnet, and perhaps, like an ill-fated catch, he will see his whole life pass before his eyes.

This is where we find Merdocai right now. It is a heartbreaking sight, but let us not turn our eyes away from his anguish. Let us keep looking. Let us stay with him so he does not feel so alone.

Chapter 7

As Teo advanced far into the woods, Rodrigo headed out, laden with wild fennel, thyme and oyster thistles.

Someday he would live where he belonged, blissful amongst the poplars, beeches, elms and cedars.

What you saw of a tree was only its half. Rodrigo knew this from those that had fallen, either from the wearying work of termites over time or a single strike of lightning in a flash. Beneath the soil, they lived a secret double life. As high as they beckoned, they penetrated as far into the earth with the curled toes of their roots. Did all things, he wondered, have hidden half-selves?

Rodrigo would not live long enough to hear the word *photosynthesis*. But he always had faith in trees as the magicians of the mysterious conspiracy of life on earth. These cogitations played in his thinking many centuries before scientists confirmed that trees take in the gaseous compound of carbon dioxide expelled through animal and insect outbreath; then, by sheer alchemy, they spin a sliver of light, rinsed with rain, into the next breath of those beholden to oxygen.

Trees trusted the ground beneath them as their only home, no matter the inadequacies of the soil on which they stood. Even if there might be more prosperous purchase beyond that mountain, where the sun shone persistently and rain fell more reliably, they did not waste a skerrick of their green energy in longing for what they did not already have. They stood where they were, forsaking wanderlust for steadfastness.

It pained Rodrigo that such mighty and magnificent beings could be reduced to the mundane on a whim. Did they ever forget the blade of an axe that cut them down for wood? Did they dream of revenge? No, he concluded. They were generous and unspiteful. But if a man could cut down a tree without weeping or begging the forest's forgiveness, there was no telling where his cruelty might lead him.

In this way, Rodrigo worried for the future of humankind.

It took a full turn of the sun and moon to cross the forest and reach the ocean – if one did not get lost. Teo knew this from Rodrigo, who sometimes vanished for days when he made the crossing. This thought comforted and then unnerved Teo as fatigue began to mount her bones.

Even with 20/20 vision (a modern term to describe what an average two-eyed person can see without the aid of corrective lenses at a distance of twenty feet) it would be a struggle to discern happenings unfolding in the begriming darkness of a timberland by the small glow of a lantern alone. So imagine, if you can, how painstaking it would be with just one eye.

Still, they trotted ever onwards, as Teo's thoughts strayed to Sancia and the progression of her fever.

'We cannot get lost, Isabel,' she said out loud. 'Do not fret or distress yourself. The stream leads to the river, and the river to the ocean. Can you smell the salt in the air?'

She wondered if Isabel was wearying, but it was better not to ask, lest she lay untoward thoughts in her goat's little head. Why speak of tiredness? Rather speak of beauty. She pointed out the velvet lichen, remarked upon the leathery smell and the twittering of jays and goldfinches. She wondered out loud whether they might spy an ibex, and who can blame her? Don't we all wish to re-encounter the magic of the past, if only to convince ourselves it was true and real after all, and not just a memory, slipping like a chimera into the eclipses of long-gone?

It was advancing on her, the realisation that they would need to overnight in the woods. Rodrigo slept in a lair he'd assembled from fallen logs, mosses and bark, but Teo had never been permitted to join him, for Merdocai forbade such risk-taking in realms where snakes and bears were rulers, and humans mere intruders.

'Danger will find you well enough. Do not go looking for it,' he'd caution, and, before he could stop himself, '… like your mama …' would slip out. Before Teo could ask a single question from the assortment that jostled on her tongue, he'd hold up his hand and say, 'That is all, Teo.'

Now in the very place her father had warned her about, Teo began to chatter wildly, which is what we sometimes do to quell trepidation. She spoke aloud to Isabel about the ghost mushroom Rodrigo had storied her with — only to be beheld in the dark, not to be touched or eaten. Could it be true that they lit up from the inside? Teo longed to see it with her own eye, though not because she didn't believe him. She'd asked a hundred hows and whys, and listened to all of Rodrigo's theories. Neither of them would ever learn of luciferin, a chemical that environmental scientists would identify centuries later, responsible for this magical happening. This is perhaps just as well, for Rodrigo would always favour the mystery over rational explanation, as all true poets do.

Isabel paused at the lip of the stream and lowered her head to quench her thirst. Teo copied her. It was good to have Isabel's caprine companionship at such a time, to help her feel at home in the world when she was so far from family. In fact, Teo could not think of a circumstance in which it was not a comfort to have a goat beside her.

'What do you make of all this?' she asked Isabel. 'I tie a rope around your neck, and you follow me. You don't worry, "Is this the right thing to do? Is this a terrible mistake?" You don't concern yourself with, "When will we get there?" or "Are we headed in the right direction?" and "What is coming from far away as the clouds are gathering strength?" Isabel, you give me such courage.'

She put her arm around the goat's neck and kissed her on the top of her head. It was a bafflement to try to understand anything at all, let alone what this treacherous quest meant to a four-hoofed animal. It didn't matter. Loving something was more important than understanding, especially loving something you couldn't quite understand.

Images of Sancia's fevered entreaty and the pox's terrifying hurtling indifference intruded into her mind, but Teo spoke to herself thus:

'Will worrying hasten your feet? No, it will likely slow you down, even cause you to make mistakes.'

She would keep going until she found Malakha, until she had a cure in her hand to bring back for Sancia. She checked her pocket to feel the note. Yes, there it was, still. Her thoughts travelled to where her father might be now. She imagined him seated on a throne, surrounded by good doctors feeding him tinctures as he offered his arms, his limbs, for The Greater Good. Surely such virtue could only summon his speedy return to them?

In this state of rumination and self-exhortation, Teo suddenly realised that, though she was fastened tight to the lantern, she had lost hold of the rope in her other hand. Isabel had disappeared amongst the be-foliaged shadows.

A small welling of anxiety rose inside her. Her goat was not one to wander far, being a *by your side through thick and thin* companion. The unfamiliar sounds in the forest suddenly sounded exaggerated, and though Teo was not fearful for the sake of it, a sense of the sinister overcame her momentarily.

'Isabel?' she called. 'Isabel, where are you?'

A rustling was followed by the goat's triumphant emergence from the dark brush. Let me describe what she had in her mouth: a feathered critter, grey, brown and white, with a spiky crest of rust-coloured feathers on the back of her head. A duckling, of all things. Isabel gently plopped it at Teo's feet. It tried to right itself, but alas, it kept falling over, leaning to one side despite its grand aspirations of waddling and fluffing and ruffling.

Teo crouched down to see better. It appeared to have some defect, by birth or accident. It made a small duckling sound, in the manner of *tweep, tweep.*

'A red-breasted merganser,' she murmured. 'Are you lost? Where is your mother?' (Which are questions that arise spontaneously when one comes across a being all on its innocent own.) 'Isabel, you have saved this dear maimed duckling. What a clever goat you are.'

Teo reached out to touch the bird, but it mistook her gesture for danger and fell further over on its side, twitching in the fear that often besets small things in the face of larger ones. She knew exactly how it felt to be motherless in a big, baffling world mamas could surely guide one through more assuredly than one could navigate alone.

Teo held out a small piece of bread and the duckling nibbled on it, hungry. Isabel nudged the bread closer to the duckling.

Then, something very small but remarkable happened: the duckling became smitten.

All things are besotted in a chain of interlinking connections. This is how life pulses onwards, in a restless, aching devotion. The mouth is smitten with the burst of the blackberry, as blackberries are smitten with the ripening sun. The sun adores the rain, which is why we have rainbows, just as the rain nestles into the laps of the forests. Each tree is a bride to the earth, while the ground hugs every lifeless animal in a disintegrating embrace.

Who could say whether it was Isabel's little beard against her feathers, or her soft eyes? Perhaps it was the smell of grass on her breath, or the bleat that erupted from her dark lips. Maybe the duckling mistook Isabel for her mother, who had laid the egg from which she had hatched in the nest of another duck, which is a rascally mischief common to mergansers. Or she determined that the nanny goat's head offered an inviting perch with a better view. We might hypothesise this way and that, but in the end, it remains a secret for only ducklings to know.

She hopped onto Isabel's head and curled between the crutches of her two horns. The infatuated duckling seemed happy, as did Isabel, which in turn made Teo happy. When we are smitten, the heart becomes full and overflows, and everyone and everything around us is touched by it.

Sometimes, an apparently insignificant but unusual event chances upon us. At the time one might remark, 'How peculiar' or 'Why on earth?', or perhaps one might not take any notice of it at all. It is only much later that one might look back with a sense of wonderment, and what was insignificant becomes significant. What seemed like nothing then, becomes everything after.

So I urge you to remember the little brown, grey and white duckling with a spiky mane of feathers, which is not at all in the nature of a red herring.

Chapter 8

Graviel Torrero gripped a bucket of slop as he traipsed down the treacherous spiral stairway in the citadel's prison. It was all he could manage to hold back the heaving nausea that rose to the back of his throat. The pain in his lower back stabbed him with every step. He had once used a hand-carved walking stick, which had eased his movements, but many years ago he had handed it to one who needed it more than he did. Not a day passed when he did not think on it, and never once did he wish it otherwise.

The bucket was filled with a swill of disgusting, filthy and appalling offal suited only for the incomprehensible digestive laxity of rats and cockroaches. It is only out of consideration that I refrain from describing the contents and stench in detail, lest it cause you to gag as Graviel is doing now. He covered his mouth with his one hand, while his other held on to the handle of the sloshing muck.

As he reached the bottom of the stairwell, a voice from within called, 'Hello? Is someone there? I am here for my children, for The Greater Good. Please, what is happening to me?'

Graviel had strict instructions not to engage with the Subject Matter.

'Do not blunder into pity,' the Marquis had instructed. 'That is weakness. Keep your mind fixed on the end goal – a cure for the pox for your wife and daughter, those worth saving.'

Graviel dropped the bucket on the ground and felt in his pocket for the key to the small flap at the bottom of the enormous steel door that shut the Subject Matter in the dungeon.

'My name is Merdocai Beneviste, and my children are Sancia and Teodoro,' the voice called. 'Please, what is your name?'

Graviel shook his head to dislodge the word that arrived on his tongue, ready to be dispatched: *Graviel.* Behind that word, a full sentence had lined up, wanting to be announced, like a sneeze or a cough:

I am Graviel Torrero, and I have a daughter, Beatris, who is six days old.

Graviel clamped his lips tight. But this gesture caused him to cough. As he wheezed, the pain in his lower back punctured him as if a knife were gashing into his flesh. He let out an involuntary yelp.

Weakness, Graviel thought shamefully. *I am showing weakness.*

For a moment there was silence. Then, from behind the steel door, came the voice of the Subject Matter.

'Are you in pain?'

This time Graviel could not constrain the word that skidded from his mouth like a slippery fish. 'Yes.' Hot tears pricked his eyes. In the many years since he had returned from the war, he had not had a moment's respite from this physical anguish. Yet neither had he ever expressed in words the truth of his agony. He had used every trick he had learned as a soldier to conquer its hold on him. He tried to asphyxiate it with willpower. Trample it with stoicism. Ignore its cries as one might a fox caught in a trap that cannot be saved. Though he was free to walk his life, he was imprisoned in the battered crime of his body.

Many years ago, he had carved a walking stick from a branch of an elm tree, with a handle in the perfect figure of a bee-eater bird with its fan-shaped wings. When he had moved with that flighted figure clutched in his palm, the war in his body seemed elsewhere, as if the stick itself, like a sturdy friend, absorbed some of the ache so that he had to bear fractionally less of it. Now, when the pain blinded him momentarily and time sent him backwards into that dark passage, he often thought of the pair of bloodied hands he'd pressed the stick into.

'Why don't you use another stick?' Taresa would implore. 'Any old stick.'

But Graviel always shook his head.

'Must you continue to punish yourself, *mi querido*?' she would ask despairingly.

This was a rhetorical inquiry, for of course Graviel intended his own penitence; it was a reminder of his weakness, a lashing for his part in the greater cruelty in which he was complicit by his silence and foolish, ineffectual interjections.

Now with a 'yes' freshly fallen from his lips, from behind the steel door Merdocai's voice emerged, soft with kindness.

'A war injury?'

Again, Graviel's words seemed beyond his control. '*Sí.*'

With the dungeon door between them, two men stood, each in his own despair. Merdocai rested his head against the door and placed his open palm upon it. On the other side, Graviel leaned against the door to get some weight off his right leg. His open palm pressed against it. Neither could see the other. Yet steel is a generous conductor of temperature, and the door felt the heat of both their hands and held them magnetically together for a few splendid moments, of which only you and I share the secret knowledge.

'I am sorry for your suffering,' is all Merdocai spoke.

Before he knew what was happening to him, Graviel felt a wet warmth from his eyes streaming down his cheeks. Those words entered his body and the knotted fists of nerve endings that seared through him, and for the briefest instant, the torment lifted. Such an expression of compassion from a stranger he was helping to brutalise all but melted the searing agony. He had respite, immediate and fleeting. How could a man with offal in a bucket and a piece of steel lodged in his lower back ever articulate such unlikelihoods, but it was so … it could not be more true, Graviel felt it: peace. Not just in his muscular frame, but in his spirit. It was as if he'd been struck by a flash of lightning that snatched the burden from his body; for a split second, he was a young man again, in a time before war had stolen his innocence and wedged its malice in his flesh.

'My name is Merdocai Beneviste. I am here for my children. Please, tell me, what is happening to me?'

These words of the Subject Matter broke Graviel's momentary reverie and shattered the spell of peace that had descended upon him. As the pain stormed his torso once more, squeezing all the lightness out of him, he hardened back into his job. He bent down, unlocked the flap in the steel door and lifted the bucket into the dungeon.

Without another word, he turned and began the long ascent up the spiral staircase, wiping the last of his tears with the sleeve of his jacket.

Chapter 9

Besides the incoming night, it is my responsibility to draw your attention to another portentous phenomenon that was slowly gathering out at sea. Weather, as we know, is not driven by its own heartache and revenge, but is only an ally or enemy of our happiness or despair. Who amongst us has not shivered with misery in a bracing wind or had our heaviness drenched out of us in a downpour? Best of all, haven't we all known the startling consolations of joy as we are warmed by the rays of the sun?

If you look out at the ocean, somewhere in the vicinity of the blue whale, you will see that all of daylight's illuminations have been dimmed, making space for the silver stint of the lunar crescent. If there is anything to know about the moon, it is that she takes her job seriously – to sing in the tides and sweeten the dark. But on this night the wind had changed direction, hauling in a drove of cumulonimbus clouds that covered her face entirely, and there was nothing she could do to shake them off. Above the ocean, warm moist air was being swept upwards, in motions invisible to any eye but with unmistakable consequences.

How much further would Teo, Isabel and the merganser be able to go as the charcoal cloak of the sky dipped low and covered all it touched?

If we go with them, we shall find out.

Isabel, wearing the duckling, stopped in her tracks. She cocked the scraggle of her ears. Her nose twitched. Teo, ahead of the goat, had already smelled it: the woody aroma of smoke.

The scent did not belong in the forest. It was not a forest fire, which the gods sometimes sent to scorch and revive the earth, but smoke rich with provisioning proposition, overlaid with singing and intermittent whistling. It was human.

Teo contemplated fear. Could this be one of the Marquis' soldiers? A hunter? A pox carrier, cast out? Did a stranger singing in a forest at night pose a danger to her? Her goat? The duckling? She placed one hand on her heart and one on her belly. The sense of threat subsided.

Thus emboldened, Teo cast a salutation in a loud voice through the shadows. 'Greetings, Whistler.'

The blathering paused. 'Who are you to name me Whistler?'

Upon hearing the voice of an old woman, Teo exhaled. 'I am called Teodoro. I was admiring the whistling, especially the trills and flows,' she called into the darkness. 'I have been practising myself but am not nearly as skilled.'

'Come closer, admirer of trills and flows,' the voice returned.

Teo and Isabel pursued the sounds and the smells, parting the understorey of shrubs and cracking twigs as they did. It seemed unlikely, but suddenly they found themselves in a clearing, where a human shape tended a small fire enclosed by a circle of rocks. A pot simmered. The smell was scrumptious and earthy.

'*Perdóneme*, Doña, for interrupting your good-smelling dinner,' Teo said in astonishment. Her belly rumbled as if it had its own life, which of course it did.

'Where are you headed, so far from home? All alone. At night. Do you not know the dark woods eat small things like children?'

'I am not a child, I have passed eleven turns of the sun. And I am far from alone. Here is my faithful goat, Isabel,' Teo said, patting her goat. 'And here is an injured merganser we have recently chanced upon.'

'A convivial goat and an ailing duckling will not protect you from the forest's hungers. If anything, you will become a three-course meal.'

Teo had no answer: the ancient hag, draped in what seemed like a cloak of pine marten and rabbit fur, was speaking nothing but the truth.

'Advance nearer,' the figure said, reaching out her left hand. Her right clutched a wooden staff.

Isabel butted in, approaching the old woman to nuzzle her arm. This was a good sign, for Isabel was a discerning ruminant and shied away from the noxious and the gruff. Teo stepped forward and, by the light of the fire, saw two empty eye sockets in the shrouded cocoon of shawls around the old woman's head. She resembled Abuela Guardiana, with fingers as gnarled and woody as twigs, that reached now for Teo's hands and climbed all the way up her arms until they touched her head, hair and ears.

'The sound and feel of a girl, but the hair of a boy. Which are you?'

Teo withdrew, her heart quickening. *Never let anyone know* ... These were her papa's words as his shears trimmed her locks, which each season grew and grew as if growing was their due. She smoothed her tunic, under which small growths were beginning to sprout. 'A boy of course ... both ... neither?'

'I see you are fond of riddles. Are you trying to trick me?'

'No, Doña.'

The old woman clucked. 'Should you not be locked behind the door of your home? What of the dreaded pox, the creeping curse?'

'I am not afraid of the pox.'

The old woman reared backwards in surprise. 'How have you escaped that fear?'

Teo paused, wondering herself. 'I have never, in all my years, suffered even as much as a small head cold.' Teo did not mean to brag. She realised that, indeed, she was not afraid for herself. She never had been.

'Are you prone to exaggerations, amplifications and embellishments? How is it possible to have never been ill? We are all of a nature to be wounded and sickened and finally ... well ...' The old woman passed her fingers across her neck and dropped her head sideways in a gruesome mime of demise.

Teo shrugged. 'It is one of the great unsolved mysteries of the world.'

'Indeed, philosophically spoken.'

'It is only what Rodrigo would say. He's my friend, you see. And I should have waited to inform him of our mission. But, alas, there was no time.'

'What else is there but time? Why the haste?'

'It is a matter of life and death.' Teo sighed.

'Ah, a mere trifle. Sit a while. Have some forest stew.'

'*Perdóneme*, Doña, but we must keep moving. Time is on my heels.'

'Life and death keep moving, in that you are correct. What is your destination? And do not speak in riddles. Tell it straight.'

Teo paused. 'I am looking for Malakha.'

The old woman went still at the sound of the name, but her lips twitched. The fire crackled in the night. 'Which tormented soul sends you to' – she paused a long while – 'Malakha?'

'My sister, Sancia, of the dark ringlets and grey eyes. She is raging sick with the pox. We have heard Malakha can relieve suffering. We are in desperate need of a cure.'

The old woman muttered, 'Come sit, child. What you are in need of is some blood-strengthening sustenance. Malakha will wait. She waits for us all. Besides, this is a blasphemous night beneath the clouds that have swirled in from the north. There will be no moon to guide you. The frogs have confirmed this. You have picked a bleak hour for your pilgrimage to the ocean, when Gota Fría is on the rise. You are bound for failure unless you stay a while.'

The old woman patted the ground next to her.

Gota Fría, oh, unlucky timing, the most violent of storms. If you came and stood in her scuffed shoes, you would feel the two directions in which Teo was yanked – one to the urgent conclusion of her assignment, the other to her exhaustion and hunger. As if to assist our young protagonist to make up her mind in this tug-of-war, Isabel sank to her knees and curled up beside the fire, the duckling tucked between her horns.

The stranger did not wait for Teo to be seated, but leaned towards the fire, scooped a metal cup into the pot and held it out. It smelled of smoke and laurel, garlic and rosemary. Teo reached for it gratefully. The old woman passed her a sackcloth of hazelnuts and Teo scooped up a handful. The old woman began to whistle again, and soft tunes fell from her gnarled mouth.

'You do not know Malakha.' The old woman said it as a statement, not a question.

Teo shook her head. 'Do you?'

'We have had many dealings in the past.'

'Can you tell me how to find her?'

The forest around them drew in, huddling closer, as if the trees were listening.

'I will not aid you in this quest.'

The soup had no trace of malice – it was sweet and woody – and so Teo's young heart was confounded.

'Why not?'

The old woman seemed unmoved by the urgency of the situation, for she rushed not at all to answer. Questions backed up inside Teo, tripping over themselves, a stampede of impatience, but she bridled them.

'You have half of understanding,' came back the gnarly reply, eventually. 'It is perhaps one of your many problems.'

Teo nodded, for indeed, she had many troubles for such a young person, and the load of them all was now beginning to bear down on her. The night's pall did not help. But the warm forest soup did. It hummed down her gullet and sank into her bones. It softened the chill inside her and brought thoughts of home, which you might imagine wasn't much, but it had traces of Sancia when she laughed and Rodrigo when he stuttered poetry and her bearded papa when he spoke softly the way a mother, if one could imagine her, might. So you could say, it was everything.

The old woman smiled at the sounds of the young girl slurping her soup. Behind the blinded barricades of her eyes, her thoughts flickered.

It is, you will appreciate, a woeful burden to hold in one's possession knowledge that others lack but need. Some brandish this discrepancy like a sword. But that is only if your language is one of conquest. What if yours is one of kindness instead?

Truth, we come to learn, is not always a blessing. It resists pursuit or hasty claims. Oftentimes it cannot be looked at straight on. Those who converse with the animals and gods are apprenticed to an appreciation of timing and patience.

Teo had not yet grasped into whose presence she had stumbled.

La Primera de los Ojos, as the old woman was known – The First of the Eyes – had gentled many women through childbirth. She had heard the name

Malakha on the lips of many birthing women who believed they were on the precipice of the Other Side. What she knew, all too clearly, was that Malakha was summoned through the hallucination of those coming to the end of their walk on earth. Why disclose to this strange girlboy that it was only those who were close to dying who ever called on Malakha?

Malakha was the name people gave to the Angel of Death.

No, this was not for the young person's hearing. The ears are the tributaries to the heart, and as one who had spent her days pulling children into this life, she was not going to poison hope or fracture the bones of those who would have to walk long after she had been laid into the cradle of the earth.

Soup was hence a reliable intermission for decelerations and adjournments to the terminal of truth.

When Teo's belly was cosied with the broth, she sighed. 'What is the other half I do not know, so that I may help my sister?'

The fire spat as the beguilements of darkness settled around them.

'Where shall we even begin?' the old woman muttered. 'With all the misunderstandings and misinformation and miscalculations and misadventures – Malakha can't save your sister.'

At this, Teo's resolve flared. 'I will convince Her.'

The old woman let out an owlish hoot. 'And what would you offer Malakha in return for Her miracle?'

Teo gulped.

'Don't tell me you are travelling empty-handed?' the old woman queried.

Apart from her scrip and her lantern, Teo's hands were certainly empty. They couldn't have been barer. She felt a small finger of doubt poking her in the ribs.

'What about the goat that walks by your side? Malakha loves a goat stew.'

'No.' Teo placed her hand protectively on Isabel's head. 'I would never part with Isabel. She is my guide, and more outstandingly, she is my friend.'

'So you would let your sister die to save your goat?'

Teo could not answer this tricky question and felt hot tears sting both her eyes – for even if you have lost one, its pouch will cry as surely as if the eyeball was still sitting happily there. Tears, it appears, have nothing much to do with eyes; they are simply the exit points for pain and confusion that arise from the heart.

'What about the duckling, maimed and unfit for its life's purpose?'

'No,' Teo said, taking in the duckling coddled contently on Isabel's head.

'You would refuse to surrender a puff of worthless feathers, a mere appetiser for Malakha, in exchange for a *miracle*?'

As the word 'miracle' fell from the old woman's breath, an emptiness gaped inside Teo. A blessing for Sancia felt as out of reach as a dream that was impossible to understand. But, Teo reasoned, if there was such magic as a miracle, surely it could not cause harm to any other living creature. How, then, could a miracle preserve its honour?

'She is part of our family now,' Teo said. 'Her name is ... well, let us give her one – Patito. I will find another way. I am carrying only a note for Malakha.'

'What is its message?' the old woman asked.

Teo shrugged. 'I promised my sister not to read it.'

The old woman settled upon this confession. 'So you are on a pilgrimage without knowing where you're going, carrying a note you have not read, to find someone you do not know, with nothing to offer in exchange?'

Suddenly Teo felt the foolhardiness of her enterprise. She wrung her hands together. 'It is so, Doña.'

'What has possessed you, child?'

Teo wondered now what had indeed taken hold of her without the chaperoning sense that such undertakings surely warrant. Had she caught the rashness of her mama, who – as her papa sometimes let slip – courted danger? But no, Sancia would never have sent her into the arms of danger.

'I trust my sister,' Teo whispered.

'Ha! That is your first mistake. A feverish pox scrambles the best of intentions.'

Teo recalled her sister's face. Her clear words. *All you need is here.*

Teo scrabbled inside her shoulder bag. Her fingers closed around the piece of trencher.

'Bread. I have bread.'

'Malakha eats flesh, not bread,' the old woman dismissed.

She fished again, and her fingers closed around her flint.

'A flint.'

'Malakha is the source of fire. She needs no flint. What else?'

Teo fumbled once more, and this time she pulled out her mother's two-tined fork.

'A fork.' Teo had all but forgotten that she had hidden it in her scrip many seasons ago, for the mere sight of it sent her sister into a breathless panic. How relieved she was to feel it between her fingers in this moment.

If the light were more generous, we might detect a change in the old woman's disposition, subtle as it may be.

'I see,' she said, which of course she could not have intended literally. 'Truly, a fork?'

'It can be used for eating,' Teo elaborated. 'Not soup, unless things are afloat.' Teo mimicked the use of the fork, but realised that no eyes, in partnership with the nighttime, made this a pointless gesture. 'It can chisel oysters from rocks.'

'I am certain that is so, for I once saw a woman do such a thing. But, child, Malakha eats rocks, not oysters. And where did you come upon such a two-tined fork with a handle of mother-of-pearl?'

Teo wondered if this was a guess or whether all forks looked like the one in her hand.

'It is a most precious artefact which belonged to my mother. The last she ever touched. It is greatly cherished by my father, but feared by my beloved sister who believes it is a bearer of bad luck.'

'And will you part with it?'

'I will give it up if only for a miracle.'

'Such as one to restore your lost eye?'

Teo gasped. 'How do you know about my eye? Forgive my observation, Doña – you have none.'

The old crone made a garrotting sound to clear her throat, before expectorating a gob of sputum onto the ground. 'You do not need them to know what is in front of you. The earthworm and the mole get along fine without them. Will you part with the Devil's pitchfork for a miracle? Speak clearly now.'

Teo knew well enough that to voice a wish was to cast a runaway spell, unspooling accidental consequences over which one held no sway. To call for rain might bring on a flood. To beg for the end of a downpour might condemn plants to bewithering and groom the ground for fire. To plead for more than one needs might deprive another of their fair share. No wish was ever one hundred per cent safe.

'My father is two fingers short of ten. Shems the gravedigger has lost his teeth; my sister, Sancia, her courage. Rodrigo speaks in stutters. I lost one eye in a fateful happenstance with a fishhook, but I have another. Why would I waste a miracle on me?'

The old woman harumphed. 'A fateful fishhook happenstance?'

'I tripped and fell against a wall as a tiny girl, and a fisherman's hook pierced my eyeball ...'

'Frog legs and ibex hooves! Who has shovelled these legends into your head?' The old woman frothed.

'It is only what my father has told me, for I was too young to remember.'

'What an imaginative liar. A concoctor of tall stories. A natterer of nonsenses,' she huffed.

Now if there was one thing Teo could not endure, it was a slur against her father.

'My papa is the most truthful and heroic of humans. He has sacrificed himself for The Greater Good. For a cure for the pox. Even for you, for you are part of The Greater Good.'

At this moment, the spume of mist from a blue whale's blowhole, five miles offshore, lifted high into the night air and came floating on the shoulders of the swirling winds, reeling in the wet warm air like fishnets. A flock of bats crossed the sky in an arc, but only the heavens could see them occluded by the billowing shawl of clouds that very night.

Miles away, Rodrigo was striding homewards with a scrip of foraged forest goods. He stopped and tilted his head to one side, as if something were trying very hard to speak through time. A rush of unease passed through him, and he began to run.

A six-day-old baby girl called Beatris, who had been restful all afternoon, began to cry inconsolably in the arms of her mother.

Deep in the chilly, callous cell, Merdocai sank into despair and began to chant the names of his wife and his two daughters.

'Who *are* you?' Teo asked, suddenly apprised of things greater than she understood.

The world grew quiet as the stranger uttered, 'They call me La Primera de los Ojos – The First of the Eyes.'

'Do I know you?' Teodoro whispered her question.

'Of course you do,' she said, holding up her gnarly fingers. 'I am one of those who saved you.'

Chapter 10

L et us leave Teo on the brink of the old woman's revelation, and rise above the forest to cast our gaze out over the mantle of ocean to where the blue whale sings.

He is headed now back to the bay of his origin. Here is where his mother had calved him eighty-nine years before, when none of the people in our story had even been born, not even La Primera de los Ojos.

In the weeks that followed, the whale's mother had lingered close to shore, nursing him in the protected waters where he could feed and rest. The villagers gathered on the cliffs and beaches to catch a glimpse of this remarkable occurrence. They felt special, even chosen, for surely it was a sign of good fortune that the mother whale entrusted the birthing of her offspring to their inlet. For weeks people chattered about nothing but whales. They lapsed into speaking of '*nuestra ballena bebé*' – our baby whale – which is a proprietary habit common to humans, to claim title to places and beings that are not, by their nature, ownable. They meant no harm by it, only belonging, and they exalted and offered thanks for many years, until the stories of the blessing of his nativity got frittered away into the galaxy of The Great Forgetting.

Now, as he travelled the thousands of miles back towards the inlet hugging the shores of Dazic, he sang his long songs, which travelled through the amphitheatre of the water to other whales thousands of miles away. He rumbled and clicked, crackled and purred, chirped and whistled. Here is where he was born and here is where he was coming to die.

He weighed 120 tonnes – equivalent to thirty elephants, if such vastness can be conceived. But in the water, he was buoyant and brilliant. He was a nomad, like all sea-homed creatures, and had traversed 800,000 miles in his lifetime, from the coldest seas of the north to the warmest parts of the tropics. Home to him was not one place, as a plot of soil tenured by a rooted tree, but the everywhereness of the waters that covered the blue planet on which he roamed.

His heart, the hugest in the animal kingdom, beat twice per minute. In the chambers of his middle ear, ossicles and membranes trembled, tailored for perceiving low frequencies underwater, such that he could detect the echoed cries and calls of other whales over a thousand miles away. He had careened alongside every swimming beast and life form from the immortal jellyfish to bottlenose dolphins, brown fur seals, sunflower starfish, weedy seadragons, small-spotted catsharks, pygmy seahorses to the leatherback sea turtle and every other ocean-dwelling fauna in between – they were all his relations. He held within him the thousands of nights when the constellations of Orion glittered above and storms no human eye had ever witnessed broke the sky with forks of silver lightning. He'd hummed beneath the lights of the aurora borealis, drunk his fill of krill and released great fecal plumes into shallow waters, rich with nitrogen and iron from sunken nutrients which, in turn, urged phytoplankton to grow and nourish other life. He'd drifted past shipwrecks and all the human disaster they held, solemn and curious and ample with wonderment.

He knew depth and distance. Suffering and longing.

He possessed the greatest lungs on earth and drew creation's deepest inhalations. He could hold his breath for almost two hours before needing to surface again. But as a mammal, to breathe, he needed to breach.

Since his birth, he had returned only once before – eleven years ago, on his way to Antarctic waters, when he had pulled into the shallower currents not far from the beaches of Dazic. Spring had almost landed, and the mackerel and cod were plentiful. Yes, he knew this place; it was filled with whale nostalgia, a wistfulness unlike the human kind, which is laden with all the many hurts of returning to a place that is unchanged, having changed oneself. In the whale's case, it was not so much a homesickness as a restoration of place to the placelessness of his nomadic life. Here a hunger for oxygen arose, and a frolic insinuated inside him. As he neared the cliffs of the west, he swung himself upwards, reeling in a huge breath, twisting in the air and landing with a gigantic splash.

In the cosmic design of many birds and sea animals, his eyes set on either side of his giant head each took in two 180-degree fields of different landscapes in a feat of eyesight known as monocular vision. Those of us with forward-facing windows to the soul cannot begin to fathom such seeing. Instead, we have binocular vision, in which each eye captures a slightly overlapping picture the brain fuses into one magical holograph.

Timing, you might be willing to concede, seems to be more a matter of fate than strategy. To be found in a location in a particular heralding moment invites meaning-making, a habit towards which humans veer – less so, whales.

And so it happened that for the briefest instant in which the whale appeared to defy gravity and scientific logic, by boosting the tonnage of his mass out of the water, his right eye caught a lone figure on a cliff, while his left spied a basket in the open water. Right then, the pattern of his life and that of another's intersected.

A whale's eyes, believe it or not, are small relative to the size of their bodies. Their pupils shrink to allow a fraction of light to enter, attuned as they are to the opacity of the ocean. They are, in truth, perhaps not the best eyewitnesses. But the auditory canals of their sharp ears miss nothing.

Whales, we might surmise, are smitten with song, hurling musical waves through the waters as they toss and turn the hull of their bodies through the ocean. It would be centuries before scientists discovered spindle cells in their brains – no different from the ones humans possess, which are entangled in the ways we love and care for others. Perhaps we can never know what a creature as elusive and mysterious as a whale can be said to 'feel' as it rides the tides and chants its dirges.

A whale's eyes, though they have no tear ducts, see both north and south, east and west.

Merdocai had always believed a whale was the sole witness to Gracia de Luna's leap into the ocean.

Yet I am here to disclose that there were others who saw it too.

One's dress was soaked from her leaking breasts and tears of regret.

The other was La Primera de los Ojos.

Chapter 11

live rabbit. Those had been his orders.

The Marquis draggled the lifeless animal by its ears. It swayed by the light of four lanterns, one in each corner of his chamber. How was Dante to be enticed with a limp lump of rabbit? The Marquis dangled the slack flop of the creature in the face of ruddy, red-headed Alfonso Rojas, his beleaguered trapper.

'It was alive when I caught it,' Alfonso offered. 'It must have died of fright. You know how rabbits are, Muy Ilustre Señor Marqués.'

In the corner of the chamber, Graviel Torrero nodded. Bunnies. Oh, he knew their tiny, terrified hearts well.

'There is only one who will die of fright if I don't get a live rabbit by tomorrow,' the Marquis threatened. 'My bird is starving to death.'

All three men turned to gaze at Dante. As they did, one of his perfect white feathers fell from a wing.

'For every future feather that drops, I will have one of your fingers. Do you understand? And I'll feed them to my hawk!'

Alfonso Rojas nodded, clicked his heels and left the chamber, a silent curse beneath his beard.

'Why am I surrounded by *torpes ineptos*? *Grandes idiotas*?' the Marquis snarled.

Graviel Torrero glanced out the window at the night sky, with a terrific longing to finally be dismissed so he might arrive at his very own front door, where he could leave his boots outside. The Marquis had been keeping Graviel later and later, every evening since the day Beatris had been born. Once? Well, one ought not jump to assign sinister intent to a solo event. Twice? A repetition, surely nothing but an echo. But thrice, and beyond? That was evidence of a tendency, more manifest as days flipped from one into the next.

'Perhaps the Marquis doesn't want to be alone,' Taresa had charitably suggested the night before, when Graviel crept in close to midnight. Happily, baby Beatris had been awake for a feed, and the day's despair sloughed off him as he felt her grasp one of his enormous fingers in her tiny possessive clasp. Nothing hurt Graviel more than to disappoint Taresa, though she was never one to add her weight to an already bruised place.

Graviel knew the malignant manoeuvres of the Marquis' mind. He would not allow others to enjoy what he could not. It was not possible, was it, could it be, that … no, Graviel did not possess the esteem to imagine it … that the Marquis might be … no, not jealous? Not of him.

On this wearying night, with a poor lifeless rabbit thrown to the floor, Graviel, desperate to be anywhere but where he was standing, blundered. 'Perhaps,' once again slid from his mouth. This was the second time in a matter of days in which he'd been unable to prevent himself from speaking just at the very moment he wished to be silent.

The Marquis turned. 'You again, with your perhapsing? Are you suffering from verbal perchance incontinence?'

'Per … haps, Muy Ilustre Señor Marqués.'

'What, Torrero, is the master plan gurgling inside that great big empty head of yours?'

Graviel was tired. No, exhausted. He was also not clever enough to pick apart the words, the tone, the slant of the Marquis' question to discern whether this was

another trap into which he would lumber. (*Gurgling* was a giveaway. It did not impress itself as a word weighted with respect.)

'The hawk, the goshawk, your albino Dante …'

The Marquis pursed his lips and closed his eyes in barely concealed impatience.

'… it's just that my father tamed an imperial eagle … as a boy, I mean …' Graviel burbled on, in a state of sleep-deprived delirium.

The Marquis began to circle Graviel as he spoke, his steel-tipped boots making a tapping sound on the stone parquetry.

'And he taught me … that is to say, he told me … that they like to …'

The Marquis halted behind the mountain of Graviel's shoulders. Graviel flinched but dared not turn.

'… hunt … on their own terms.'

From behind him, Graviel heard the slow clap of the Marquis' hands. Was it a praising or mocking applause? He closed his eyes, wishing against his own nature that he could seal the small gap that allowed the betrayal of his perhapses to slip out. There was a word he dared not utter, but which he knew to be true. Dante was *homesick*. He longed for the sky.

'Perhaps,' the Marquis bit, 'you are unable to observe that he is too sick to hunt "on his own terms"?'

He might have been weary, and therefore would never swear to its truth, but Graviel imagined it was the voice of a small, panicked boy at his back. As he summoned the vestiges of his strength, and barricaded the exits to all his perhaps-mishaps, he found those words coiling through his large head, *on his own terms, on his own terms*, and wondered if perhaps it fitted a man's life as much as that of a hawk.

Chapter 12

In her sickbed, Sancia was atremble with fever and chills. Were her symptoms caused by the bacterium *Yersinia pestis*, derived from the bite of an infected flea which spawned the Bubonic plague centuries before? Or was this the somatic anguish of regret and despair at having sent her sister away? Without a doctor to confirm either way, we can only dabble in the vagaries of speculation.

Fragments of memory pierced her like a thousand needles. Watch now, as she remembers the day she lost her courage.

She and her mama, Gracia de Luna, are out in the wide fields, collecting wild strawberries. Her fingers are sticky-red with the juice of many sweetnesses that never make it into the woven basket through which her mama's arm is slung. Sancia's mama holds her fork, which she uses to spear berries and pop them into her daughter's mouth. Her mama is singing one of her made-up songs. When her mama sings, Sancia sings.

When her mama laughs, Sancia does too. Whatever her mama dreams passes into Sancia, for that is the way of a mother and her child. They live as if in one form, even if they have not come from the same physical body. That is what love does – when a child is longed for, and adored by eyes that convey *you are wanted*, there is no 'me' and 'you', only 'we'. In this heaven, Sancia grows like a sunflower.

Golden is the thread of this memory, and it fills her with warmth like sunshine-ripe strawberries in her mouth. It is this sweet taste with which Sancia is smitten.

Her mama puts Sancia's hand on her belly, which is finally holding a brother or sister for her. How long her mama has waited for this. Sancia loves to rest her head against the small bulge and whisper words of salutation; there is only happiness in her ear, against her cheek, in the nest of her mother's lap.

'Look, Chi-chi.' Her mama points to where a swarm of swifts are swooping across the sky. Sancia turns her eyes upwards, and the world becomes filled with their calls. The swifts dance and chase each other, an enchantment to the air, sun-drenched froths of airborne wonder. Sancia's neck bends as she follows the swirling acrobatics, and her watching becomes praise of this joy for all to see.

All of a sudden, her mama lets out a howl that pierces right through the sky and the curling wonderment of ten thousand wings. '*Madre de Dios*,' she cries out as she clutches her stomach.

'Go call your papa, my Chi-chi-la,' she weeps.

Her mama falls to the ground, and her singing is gone.

Sancia turns and begins to run on her little legs. 'Papa, Papa, come quick.'

The birds continue to plunge and freewheel, but now they are ominous; their calling becomes shrill, their voices drown out her cries.

No matter how fast she runs, or how loudly she calls, until her voice is hoarse, nothing can stop the blackening around her. The sky swirls and her mama is crying in a field, and her papa is out on his fishing boat, far from shore.

Sancia runs all the way back to the village and returns with Tía Clara. Her little feet are muddy and scratched, and her heart is hammering in her chest.

When Sancia and Tía Clara reach her mama, she is curled up in a ball, whispering, 'Only Malakha can help me now.'

'Hush,' Tía Clara says. 'No, it is not time for Malakha. We need La Primera de los Ojos.'

'Malakha has already been,' Sancia's mama sobs. 'And She took my child.'

After they buried that came-too-soon baby, her mama was never able to fall pregnant again and over the long days which became longer months, Sancia watched as the bright stars in her mother's eyes dimmed.

In that moment, when Sancia saw her mother sink to her shins, the earth fell away from under her. Until then, she had never felt fear, for her mama stood like a fortress between her and the rest of existence. But when you are only small, and the person who holds your world together crumples in the same moment as a gust of wind brings a flock of birds across the afternoon sky, when the light is slanted just so and a fork drops from your mother's hand, a ghost slithers into your thinking. It whispers that you should – forever onwards – tremble at the coming dusk, wither when the wind blows and quiver at the sight of birds. It tells you that the fork is cursed. In the warp and weft of your budding mind, the threads get crossed, and all manner of things loom and lunge, threaten and terrorise.

It is a most unlucky confluence to be caught in such a muddle of tangled strands, for no-one ever chooses to be afraid of life. Fear shrivels us; it makes us even smaller than we are. Since that day, Sancia had lived her whole life as a terrified child who had failed her mama and the baby. If only she had run faster. If only she had taken a shortcut. If only she had found her papa. Maybe she could have held back the tide that upturned all their lives.

Stories are slippery in small minds and make twisted patterns in the human soul. Knots as tight as nooses.

She was the curse upon her family.

She did not have the pox. She *was* the pox.

Chapter 13

Behind the citadel's high walls and turrets, in a scant and fitful sleep, the Marquis dreamed of his mother.

She was striding ahead of him in a field of corn, and he was running after her. He followed the sound of her whistling. He wished she would turn around so he might look upon her face, but all he could make out was her back and the way her cape trailed behind her in the wind.

'Keep up, Luciano,' she shouted into the wind. *Luciano*, that was the name she had given him. How curiously it returned in the murk of slumber.

But no matter how hard his little legs tried, one weak and frail, he kept falling behind.

'Mama, Mama, wait,' he wailed. It was hopeless to run with a stiff leg several inches shorter than the other. She was not slowing down. Soon he could no longer hear her whistling; it had disintegrated into the screams of the imperial eagle and the ticking of cicadas.

The corn grew higher and higher until his mother disappeared entirely from his sight behind a wall of dense stalks.

'Mama, wait for me,' he cried, collapsing, his little palms muddied, his cheeks sodden.

Right at this moment is when he would always wake, cold with sweat, shivering, and alone, dazed and bewildered by the emptiness of the enormous bed he occupied, laden as it was with the ostentatious extravagance of silken sheets spun by silkworms from the East.

Someday it would be shared with the shape and form of a wife. Her hair. Her fingers, her thighs, her eyes and all her other mysterious parts.

In the interim, a man fated for greatness had to forgo such distractions. Matrimony and the husbandry of offspring devoured a man's freedom and cauterised his feats; they were anything but accomplishments of brainpower or strategy. Any fool could copulate and breed. Even vermin. Especially vermin. Show him one empire built on domestic foundations.

Someday, *ciertamente*, he would take a marchioness to stand beside him. She would need to be of slight stature, so as not to stand taller than he prevailed in his boots and by such inadvertent increments look down upon him. Some nights, his unbidden thoughts settled around the image of Valentina with the tresses of honeyed hair, the mistress of his half-brother, Diego, who had once smiled in his direction when he greeted her. It had been a genuine smile, of this he was confident. She had been the perfect height, and perhaps possessed of the perfect features, those lips, of course … *Diablos*, where was she now? How could a person vanish? Why had she not presented herself after Diego's death to be plucked by him from her grief? Oh, the pluckings he had in mind for her …

No importa. Before long, buxom admirers would be stampeding the citadel to win his affections. But the cursed age was against him. The pox needed eradicating. Then, oh, he would launch an experiment to end all experiments to secure himself a wife. Bosoms, buttocks and bellies came in all shapes and sizes, and why not make a feast of it? Some would be more adept with their tongues than others. Some would moan, others might shriek or shimmy. He would feast on oysters in preparation. All it would take was a tinctured aphrodisiac to sample an array of objects of desire, one each day over a full turn of the moon.

Already he had devised the invitation in his mind:

ARE YOU AN OBJECT OF DESIRE TO
PLEASE THE MARQUIS?
SENSUAL Experiments
ONE HUNDRED PER CENT Safe.
SUBMIT YOUR BODY
For the Marquis' Pleasure
Reward: The Marquis, of course

Thus, did the Marquis dream of the fabulous, sensuous life he was owed, in fitful, frantic fantasies.

But whenever he startled from his nightmares, in the vacuum of darkness, he thought to himself that anyone would do. Just another warm human body beside his mangled one, to grasp his hand and touch his cheek and whisper, 'There, there, Lazaro. All things will be well in the light of a new day.'

Deep in the dungeons below the high tower, another man woke in a cold sweat, shivering and alone for reasons that could not be more different. Who would come to save him? No-one who cared about him knew where he was.

This was the depleting wave that kept breaking over Merdocai, pulling him under. He had all but put himself in prison. Who could be so foolish as to fall into such a trap? He had always been a careful and learned man, who trusted in goodness and justice, but now his faith had been stretched to breaking point.

The bucket shoved once a day through a small flap at the bottom of the door could not be stomached by any human. He would die there, of starvation and remorse, leaving his daughters orphaned and alone.

Merdocai sat curled in a corner, possessed only of thoughts of Sancia and Teo.

'Forgive me,' he wept. 'Forgive me.'

At this same late hour, Graviel was slumped across his horse, Sombra, finally released by the Marquis from his duties. Mobilised perhaps by his sorrow for the albino goshawk, a memory from far away made its way back to him now, as his mare's hooves clipped the stones of the cobble streets.

All boys have their hunting stories and, if a man grows as he should, he will return to his with a pageant of heartache, as Graviel did on his way home this night. He had once, without now being able to summon the rationale for it, shot a bird in the long grasses with a slingshot, perhaps only out of boredom but more likely as a contorted cry to gain his father's attention. It was a bee-eater, he discovered when he ran to find it where it fell. One wing was snapped, and it flopped to the side of its body like a flag without wind. The cries it emitted stoned him in return.

He'd wrapped its warm body in his jacket and taken it home, where he'd kept it in the barn of his homestead. To this hospice of remorse, he returned each day with earthworms, seeds and caterpillars he collected in the woods. But a bee-eater needs bees, and little Graviel (who was never in truth very little), as much as he attempted, could never catch them.

'Put it out of its misery,' his father instructed. 'Its flying is over. Snap its neck. Show mercy.'

Graviel had no words to explain his failure to follow his father's instructions, except that it seemed his whole life somehow hung there in the balance of his being able to restore life to the blue, yellow, green and brown feathered bird. But no matter how attentively he took care of it, the creature withered and died, just as his father predicted.

Sometimes Graviel thought of that bee-eater and wondered if he was no different. Something needing to be put out of its misery. Something that would never fly again.

Each one of us has our own turmoils. When they come, it is easy to forget that there is never a moment when we are utterly abandoned, even if we feel it to be so.

If we return to the cell in which Merdocai finds himself, though starved and afeared, he is undeniably who he has always been — a man of merit and honour, even if he can not see it.

Perhaps it is due to the shortcomings of human vision, but it is more likely woven into the tapestry of secret patterns: what he could not perceive in this hour of despair is that there are times when a man will fall to his knees, only to give another the chance to rise to his greatness.

Chapter 14

Let us take leave of these two men in their hours of suffering, while we invoke the annals of another's sorrow, no less heartbreaking, nor random, no matter how it first appears. For perhaps, if storytelling can be trusted at all, it might, in the roundness of time, seal a loop we didn't even realise was for closing.

Gracia de Luna had always dreamed of babies. Ever since she was a sniff of a little girl and Paloma, her pet duck, had a brood of her own. Gracia carried the jittering balls of fluff around in the pocket of her apron. She let them nestle under her chin. She swam them on the ponds. She was, one might infer, smitten with diminutives.

Each of us hopes for something beyond the day-to-day curvatures of circumstance and millstones of obligation. Gracia's dream was to become a mother. She trained by helping her mother, Dionora, with her five younger siblings, lullabying them to sleep in her brown arms and peek-a-booing them out of tears and into giggles. As she grew into a young woman with wide hips, she would often place her hands upon her soft belly, as one might consecrate a home to keep its inhabitants safe and warm.

After her modest wedding to Merdocai, in which they pledged their vows to eternity, the time finally came for her to grow her own family. She tried. But none was able, like a barnacle or oyster clasped on a rock, to hold on to her. On the few occasions that one did, it fell away too soon, like a hand losing its grip on a branch. Weeks and months passed, and they kept slipping from her, four, five, six times. When a longing one has held so dear begins to slip away, a person can tumble headlong into an abyss of despair. Allow me to confide that it took every shred of strength inside Gracia to keep facing the morning sun and singing upstream for a miracle.

Her body was like a leaky boat, and nothing she ever did could keep a baby from seeping out of her. Merdocai grieved not only for their despair, but for the vacancy in Gracia's eyes, which confessed that with every precious parcel she dropped, she trusted herself less and less as worthy of conveyancing new life.

'I will make you a tea of turmeric and ginger,' Clara whispered to Gracia.

'Sardines are the best for a baby,' the fishmonger's wife advised.

'Plant sunflower seeds in the spring,' the old wives murmured.

'Ask the gods to forgive your sins,' a neighbour with five healthy children suggested triumphantly, for aren't there always those who take a strange delight in the troubles of others?

Gracia followed each of these titbits of advice, but to no avail.

You must know that, even though she lived all this time with a heart that kept shattering a little more with each loss, she never stopped hoping and wishing to become a mother.

Who knows why she began to sing to the whales? Is it because they have always been signs of promise, messengers of hope? Perhaps she believed they were wise and ancient enough to have seen all manner of human despair, and it made her feel less alone to imagine they were holding her tiny dream with her.

Each morning, in the dark before dawn, she woke with Merdocai and accompanied him down to his fishing vessel. Once his boat was nothing but a speck in the distance, as the first rays of sun were tinkering with the horizon, she would find a place beyond the comings and goings of the fishermen, stand with her toes in the water and sing. It was a call that came from deep inside her – melodies full of enigma and the struggle of beauty to be weighted with life. She let out strains of something trying to make its way through the crease of history into the here and now – a plea for mercy, for the gift of aliveness.

If you have longed for something this much, perhaps you too have found yourself doing improbable things, for there are no right and wrong ways to wish.

Sometimes when her eyes were lifted to the sky, she could hear the whales singing back. 'Yes, it will come to the one who waits longest.'

Then, two years after their marriage vows, Clara arrived one morning clasping a newborn baby girl whose unmarried mother had tragically died in childbirth. Gracia was right there, a mother-in-waiting. She grasped her in thanks and covered the baby girl with kisses.

'We will call her Sancia.'

Finally, she and Merdocai became a family.

When there is an abundance of rainfall and the heavens open wide, the rivers guide the water to the ocean, where it becomes part of the common enlivenment. The adoration in Gracia's soul that had dammed up inside her, never having anywhere to flow, suddenly knew the way. She showered all her pent-up devotion on Sancia. She rocked her in safe arms, fell asleep with the child's cheek against hers and sang made-up nursery songs. The little girl sprouted like a beanstalk in great gusts of glorious girlhood. She twirled, she smiled, she mimicked, she made mud pies; the stones she collected clinked like musical notes in her tiny hands. She flourished, rising from the misfortune of her birth to become the beloved daughter of two parents who loved each other.

It wasn't that Gracia was greedy. Mothering Sancia quenched Gracia's longing – almost. But it also had an unforeseen consequence – it roused all the tenderness within her, causing love to overflow, because that is the way it goes. It is the very opposite of meagreness. It begets more, the more you give it away.

Gracia could not let go. She knew she was destined for more children.

'We must be grateful for what we have,' Merdocai kept reminding her. 'Look at this wonderful child, aren't we glad for her?'

'We are gladder than glad,' Gracia agreed. 'We could not be gladder if we were offered a thousand doubloons to purchase the largest *barca* ever made by a human hand, with a keel and a pointed bow and stern so you could fish in deeper waters.'

But you know that feeling, do you not, where your hunger has been fed but there is still a space that has not been filled – most likely for something sweet? It was this vacancy that Gracia woke with each morning, like a prophecy in her blood. It was a secret she whispered when she was all alone, and only to the whales.

With every kiss she planted on her daughter's forehead, with every slumbering caress they shared, Gracia's bid for another child grew; it began low, but it rose to a frothing wildness that churned inside her like the ocean itself.

It is a painful utterance, but it must be said. It made her reckless.

Chapter 15

Graviel Torrero removed his tight-fitting helmet. He could almost feel his skull sigh and pop back from its constriction as he wrenched it off like a shoe too small for the foot that wears it. His large head, free at last. He folded his pants and jacket at the foot of his bed, and slipped on his loose-fitting tunic. As he did so, the weight of the day slipped off him.

The smell of warm stew wafted into the bedroom, filling him up after a day of being siphoned empty by the Marquis' demands.

He was not equal to the Marquis, of course. Not by education and rank. It was no secret – he had struggled at school. Learning to read had been a bafflement. And writing, oh, what torment. He had been punished more times than he could count for penning letters the wrong way around. He always drew his Ps and Ds and Bs and Rs and Ss in reverse, as if they'd turned their backs on the words they had found themselves in, as if they were as lost as he was. No matter how diligently he concentrated, his brain simply couldn't instruct his hand to move in the right direction. As he received the strap to his bungling fingers yet again, he wondered who had decided that a B should have its straight spine to the left and its loops to the right. To him, a B was as much a B whether it faced one way or the other. Well, a boy such as this learns to be called an oaf, a *bobo*, a fool, *estupido idiota*. He'd left school, unable to finish, and became a soldier.

He had fought in a war. He had run through a hail of fire and made it back safely. Many a night he wondered if the blade lodged in the base of his spine, which caused him eternal pain and distracted his mind from any task, had been worth a life going forward.

Now all he had to do was look in the face of his child, and he knew it was.

As he bent to take off his shoes, the words of the Subject Matter rang in his ears. *Please, I am here for my children. Please, what is happening to me? I am here for The Greater Good. What is this torture?*

At the very least, the man was owed a reason for why he was being fed inedible swill. An explanation. Surely that wasn't treason?

He cast his thinking back several weeks, to the day the Marquis had explained his Genius Plan that had come to him late at night when he could not sleep.

Was it not the case that rats and cockroaches survive all famines, illnesses and disease? Were they not the hardiest of all living creatures? The most difficult to exterminate?

Graviel had nodded, without understanding that this was an ambush.

'So the answer must lie with these vermin,' the Marquis had pronounced. 'If we can force a human to consume what these creatures do, we will understand what strengths a human body can muster. Is that not so?'

Graviel's eyes grew wide. 'Er ... *sí*, *sí* ... Muy Ilustre—'

The Marquis had cut him short. 'A doctor. We need one to verify this hypothesis. Torrero, gather Dispensables from the slums. For experimentation. A hundred or so. Sufficient for comparative analysis.'

Now, you are apprised of the fact that Graviel wasn't an educated man. And perhaps there was a certain logic to the Marquis' plan. But Graviel had what the Marquis didn't. A gut. A feeling.

That something about all this was ... wrong.

But he could not find words to explain this feeling. Just feelings.

He was losing his edge.

He was becoming soft.

It was his daughter. Her eyes.

He shuddered as the thought presented itself: he had more in common with the poor wretch in the cell than he did with the Marquis.

Graviel wasn't one to question his superiors. That sort of insubordination would get a soldier into trouble. You were given orders, and you followed them. Some men were born to give instructions, others to execute them. Graviel understood that he was an executioner. He tried to sluice the sloshing of these unruly meditations.

All it had taken was to summon Doctor Ignacio Tramposo, who had once before performed a deplorable deed for the Marquis. Self-nominated as Medico de la Peste, the Plague Doctor, he was quick to 'scientifically' back the Marquis' plan in return for gold doubloons. Doctor Tramposo had lost more patients than a physician could reasonably be expected to remember, given the numbers. He did not call the sick by their names, but by the trials in which he enrolled them without their knowledge or consent. 'Research precedes recovery,' he would repeat when families questioned why their loved ones had succumbed to conditions that only befell them after he had begun to treat them.

He raunchily echoed the Marquis' words in a formal document, signed before state witnesses, propping up the Marquis' hypothesis with medical terms in a language Graviel did not understand:

Heretofore … anatomia … cardiacus … phlegmatic … sanguine … miasma … phlebotomy … purgation.

Though he couldn't spell these words, each one struck a note of sheer dread in Graviel, for a man has only to be inadvertently roped into an act of bloody cruelty once to understand the personal precipice on which certain engagements teeter.

On this night of our story, though it was long past the eating hour, Taresa waited for her leviathan of a husband. She kept a lantern lit at the window so that, from afar, it glowed like a lighthouse in dark storms, guiding him back.

'It is not home until you're home.' She smiled as he entered.

As he sat down beside her at the table, she asked him how his day had treated him, and whether he was still in pain. A medley of particular words gathered illicitly on his tongue. No matter how he tried to swallow them down, they refused to disperse. And so, what he found himself uttering to the woman he loved was, 'One of the poor has volunteered to become the Subject Matter of a human experiment. So we might find a cure for the pox.'

Taresa nodded, causing her hair to shimmer by the light of the lantern. She was caramel in the bitterness of life. Her eyes coaxed further rebels from his lips.

'But the Subject Matter has been locked up like a prisoner and is being fed manure and rotting shit – fit only for rats and cockroaches.'

Taresa shook her head quietly. Her ringlets curled at her shoulders. Such shoulders. 'Eat before it gets cold,' she encouraged.

Graviel took a bite of the warm stew. He felt pure life rushing into him. He chewed and swallowed.

'The Marquis believes, that is to say ... it is his ...'

'... hypothesis?' Taresa offered.

'... yes, hypothesis ... that we will discover the secrets of vermin who outlive all diseases. And in this way, he says ... we will learn the secrets to health.'

Taresa did not speak. She looked up as if she were absorbed in reflection.

'I am no genius. I have a small brain for such a big head, not much between the ears, not the sharpest tool in the foundry ... but am I right in thinking ...' Graviel began. 'Is that ...'

'Nonsense?' Taresa finished.

Graviel breathed out a huge sigh of relief.

'Nonsense,' Graviel repeated.

'Gibberish,' Taresa added.

'Gibberish,' Graviel echoed.

'Claptrap, babble and drivel,' Taresa continued.

Graviel chuckled. Taresa too.

There, across the small table between a man and his wife, amongst mouthfuls of hot, warming food she had prepared, with their newborn daughter asleep in the cot and a fire blazing in the grate, Graviel was nourished. The feelings stifled inside him whenever he put on his tight-fitting uniform were finally freed. He could speak truthfully and wholesomely.

As a soldier, he'd run through the spears and axes of war once before. What he knew in the peace of this moment is that he would put his body on the line again to protect his daughter if it ever came to it. The poor man shackled in the cell in the citadel had shown him that part of himself again. He was doing just that for his children.

'I ... admire the Subject Matter's ... courage.'

That small word landed like a bee-eater on the table between their two bowls of stew.

Its discharge from Graviel was anything but a salute in a tight-fitting helmet or the firing of a cannon on command. There are first times for everything, which herald a break from the past and the beginning of an aliveness never known till now. This was the first quiet disruption to one man's history of never thinking for himself.

The word did not bark, and it did not jump. It glowed luminous in a darkening time.

Taresa looked her husband squarely in the eyes. 'Let us call him by his true name.'

Graviel nodded. 'Merdocai Beneviste.'

Chapter 16

The moment his name was uttered by Graviel Torrero, Merdocai sat upright in his cell.

'Hello?' he spoke into the darkness. 'Is someone there?'

After many days deprived of all light, sleep, and food fit for human consumption, Merdocai's dreams seemed more real than the bleak and ruinous tomb in which he found himself.

By now, the rats, mice and cockroaches scampered around and over him, undaunted by his human presence. In this pandemonium of skittering and scratching, Merdocai fell into a meditative trance as his eyes adjusted to the shadows and his senses acclimatised to those of his cellmates. He studied how roaches ran away from the light of the lantern when the slop was delivered. They came alive in the darkness, purposeful and industrious. In the moments when he could properly observe them, Merdocai's brain became busied with a thousand unanswered thoughts: could they survive without their heads? If so, how did they breathe? How fast could they run? How was it possible to squeeze through an aperture so much smaller than the size of one's body? Did they feel loneliness? Were they as repulsed by humans as humans were by them?

As for the rats and the mice, what did they communicate when they looked into each other's eyes? Did they wink and give their word and tell tales of a long day of scavenging? Could they bore one another? Did they dread the lurch of a cat and fear being blinded and having their tails cut off with a carving knife? Did they calculate time and wonder what the tick-tock of a clock meant? Could they inspire one another to greatness? Were there leaders and followers amongst them, the lucky and the hapless, princesses and royalty? Were they prone to longing for autumn and admiration of one another's whiskers and worries about a sick child? Did they ever look up and admire the clouds? Did they have welcoming anthems and risk speaking their truth? Could they aspire to heroism? Was it possible to teach them another language? Did they plot and scheme, and could you tell by looking at their expression what nefarious thoughts were skittering through their minds?

Curiosity is a kind of light, which eagles the spirit. It is the enskyment of the self, no matter the confinement of the body.

Beyond their differences, he recognised their similarity. Everything tried so gallantly to survive. He was glad for the company of other living beings. They lessened his loneliness. Would you believe, they gave him hope? In this way, his fear and antipathy disappeared.

'Hello,' he finally uttered. 'I'm Merdocai. We might as well make friends.'

Without nourishment over days, Merdocai began to hallucinate. A quiet flood of memories rose up in him, like that time a billowing of jellyfish bobbed to the surface of the water in the days when he had been a fisherman. In that other existence.

He remembered the first music he had ever heard as a boy, played on a *viola da gamba*, and how it had claimed his blood like a passionate seizure.

He saw clearly again how, one wintry day at sunset, a flock of starlings whirled in a murmuration across a grey, storm-bearing cloud, their tens of thousands of wings a low fluttering thunder through the dense haze. And how a falcon then swooped into the moving sculpture, a dark murdering shadow. All in one moment, Merdocai had grasped beauty and terror, and how they were one feeling that moved like that cloud of birds through his soul.

He recalled the life he had left behind, and for the first time he felt the ache he held inside him that yearned for the ocean. It rolled before him, in great tussling waves – the truth, that he had lived without his beloved for eleven years, and it still felt hollow in the place she once occupied inside him. That emptiness was her empire, entirely Gracia's, never to be ceded or usurped or colonised by another.

He thought of the geometry of creation and how Teo had burst, like those bright starlings against an oncoming storm, into the wasteland of his grief, and had broken open a secret door inside him he hadn't even known was there.

Oh how he missed his girls. Sancia, who cared for her sister like a mother, and Teodoro, whose rightful name was Dorotea, if the way of things had been proper and righteous. She knew how to witness every astonishment under the sun and moon with her single eye and, to her, one question was simply a door that led to the next. Just to hold them both in his mind's eye – which is a secret chamber of seeing, far from the limitations of optical constraint – suffused him with sustenance. They were with him, right there, despite the unbridgeable divide between them.

He thought of how the night calls forth the stars and wondered if he'd ever see such glory again. He wept at how intensely he loved those stars, maybe as much as he had adored Gracia, as much as he loved Sancia and Teo. His spirit became heavy with all his errors and shortcomings, including his failure to never sing his thanks just for them being there.

What we have here, as this chapter draws to a close, is a man undone by all he has lost, who begins to chant a hymn of praise with nothing more than an audience of rodents and parasites to witness it. It is an enumeration of all the things he loves and all the things he did not know he loved until now. It echoes off those cold dungeon walls and descends upon every listening creature within earshot, with the tender touch of a blessing.

Chapter 17

We return now to the small room in which Sancia lay trembling, all on her own. The fever that had consumed her had dipped, and in its place, a chill had taken over, so that her bones had turned to icicles. She called out, 'Papa,' but then she remembered he was gone for The Greater Good.

'Mama, I am so cold,' she sobbed, but then she recalled her mama had been swept away by the dangerous ocean and, oh, how she needed the touch of a mother's hand on her forehead.

'Teo,' she croaked. But the room was compressed by shadows, without even the faint remnants of the glimmering hearth Teo had lit earlier in the day. Sancia began to whimper.

What had she done? How far would Teo have gone by now? Had fear caught up with her? What if she, with her limited vision, had trodden on a ladder or viperine snake? Would the wolves, lynxes and wildcats keep their distance? Why had she thrust her Teo into such treacherous unknowns? And how long would it take for her sister's curiosity to overcome her, and cause her to open and read the note? Sancia only hoped that by the time Teo realised she had been tricked, and turned to come home, she – Sancia – would be dead, swept into the arms of Malakha, the dark angel hovering above her. Perhaps by then their papa would be back with them, and a cure would have been found. It would be too late to save her, but not too late to save Teo.

She'd had no choice. She had to send Teo away.

Well, what would you do if you loved someone as much as Sancia loved her sister?

What if Teo caught the pox from her? Then they would both be gone. But Teo had to survive. She'd already survived once.

Sancia curled up and sobbed into the gloom, made emptier by the absence of everyone to whom she mattered at all.

In her delirium, Sancia remembered the day her mama was taken by the sea.

She had only been a little thing herself, no more than five years old, when the antennae of memory were just beginning to twitch. Tía Clara had been teaching her to count with pebbles and potatoes and Sancia's little brain was buzzing and whirring.

'One, two … *uno*, *dos*.' Clara smiles, placing a stone in one of her palms and a potato in the other.

'One, two …' Sancia repeats. Big, brown and warm; small black and cold, but they sit in her hands with the same weightiness.

'*Dios mío* … what is this …?' Clara inhales, as she looks up and shields her eyes from the sun.

There comes a man, stumbling up the hill, a bundle in his arms. Something about his hunched stagger causes the potato, then the stone, to dislodge from Sancia's hands. They fall onto the ground, *plop*, *plop*. His head is bowed, and … he is trailing water, it drips off him. Even a small girl who is learning to count knows that these do not add up to a usual homecoming day. Something is unright, ominous … like a baby falling from a mama's lap … like the world shaking and breaking. He emits sounds she has never heard before. Noises with no words. The sun is shining but Sancia is cold. The flesh on her arms and legs prickles.

Tía Clara rises to her feet and the potatoes and pebbles fall from her apron onto the dust, bumping against each other. She stumbles towards the man and his bundle.

Tía Clara's cries of, '*Dios mío*, no, no, no …' land in Sancia's eyes before her ears, as if her voice is displaced from what is happening before her. Sancia's fingers squeeze a hard pebble on the ground.

The man lurches and crumples beside her, still holding his burden.

'Mama is gone, my Sancia,' he sobs. And this is how she knows this is her papa.

He looks up, with a face that is not his but a distorted contortion that has latched onto his features.

The world spins on its axis. Sancia gets to her feet and totters backwards. 'I will go find her, Papa.'

Her papa groans in grief. 'Ah, *mi querida* ...' He shakes his head. '*Es irreparable* ... too late.'

But he doesn't know how fast she can run. She has learned to go faster and faster since that day.

Then, a cry emerges from his bundle and her papa pulls back a blanket to reveal a little monkey face. One eye is open, the other is red and swollen. It is the ugliest face Sancia has ever seen.

'Mama tried to save it,' he sobs.

'*Dios mío*,' Tía Clara whispers, placing her hand on Sancia's papa's shoulder.

In this moment, Sancia cannot grasp the utmost loss and the greatest gift all at once, like a potato in one hand and a pebble in the other. It is too much for a small girl to bear. Papa takes her hand and brings it to touch the face of the baby in his arms. It is soaked. But at Sancia's touch, it stops crying.

'You have the magic touch,' Tía Clara says, patting Sancia's head. Sancia looks at her own fingers, which are not the same anymore because now they are magic.

'Is it a boy or a girl?' Sancia asks.

Papa shrugs. '*No se*, I don't know …'

'Is it ours?' Sancia whispers.

His shoulders heave and shudder. He reaches out to touch Sancia's face.

'*Sí, sí*, it is yours,' Tía Clara says. '*Indudablemente.*'

Sancia looks back at the baby. It is the most beautiful face she has ever seen.

With the shock of Gracia lost to the ocean still shrieking through his veins, Merdocai had steadied at Clara's words. Life's way was to take with one hand and give with the other. Gracia had yielded hers to try to save this small person, delivered to his arms by tragedy alone. What his daughter needed now was a pillar she could count on.

'Yes, *mia cariño*, it is our miracle,' Merdocai wept. 'A gift from God.'

'Teodoro,' Clara whispered, 'if it is a boy. Dorotea if it's a girl.'

The baby's one eye blinked and blinked, and then something extraordinary happened. It smiled and let out a small but undaunted sound we call a 'coo'.

'Teo,' Sancia whispered. 'A gift from God.'

Everything had ended then.

Sancia had inherited a sister, they soon discovered. But wisps of gossip on the tongues of villagers terrified Merdocai. 'Witch's baby.' 'Did not drown, but floated.' And, 'Who took it in?' The rumours of Gracia's death rumbling through Dazic were laced with undulating menace.

Days later, Merdocai had packed up his family and, in the quiet of a moon-filled night, they'd made the silent and arduous journey through the forest to the village of Vilingraz, from which there was no view of the ocean, not even a glimmer from the highest vantage point. Clara had wept at this parting, and so had Sancia. The sea was left behind along with Merdocai's life as a fisherman.

With the baby's head wrapped in muslin, Clara showed Sancia how to change the dressing over her eye when it soaked through. She remembered the way the water in a bucket turned pink from the blood and how she laid out muslin in the sun to dry.

'Teodoro, we will call this baby,' Merdocai instructed. A boy by day, a girl by night. A boy to all but him and Sancia.

In Vilingraz, he paid a woman who had just given birth to her sixth child to be a wet nurse for the first few months of Teo's life, so she might grow as babies need to.

Though she was just a child herself, Sancia had carried the little one in her arms and strapped her on her back to lilt her to sleep. Teo reached her fingers out to touch the hair, the smile, the nose of the one face she knew was her safe home. Sancia fed her goat's milk with a horn. When she could sit alone, Sancia spooned mashed potatoes softened in milk into Teo's mouth.

When Teo grew into a toddler and out of her crib, they shared a bed. Sancia, remembering the stories her mama had told her, spoke them into Teo's baby ears, and in this way she learned to speak. They say blood is thicker than water, but that is because they never came across such siblings-by-circumstance as these.

Teo's first word was 'Sun', for Sancia, then 'Why?' and then 'How?' and then 'What?' and then 'Where?' Between them, Merdocai and Sancia struggled to keep up with the questions that flew from her mouth like bees on reconnaissance, returning hive-bound to assemble the silent honeycomb of her thoughts. With every inch of height she reached, the wingspan of her questions grew.

'Mama' was a word Sancia taught her – a fable about where babies come from. Teo learned that she was the child of Gracia and Merdocai, and that the sea had stolen her mama when she was days old. Only Merdocai and Sancia knew that Gracia had never held, met, nor touched Teo. Now you and I know it too.

'Do not tell her how it came to be, Sancia,' Merdocai whispered. 'She will be troubled to learn that it was in trying to save her that your mother was taken by the sea. Let her live unsaddled, free.' Merdocai had grasped Sancia's little hands in his and brought one of his eight fingers to his lips.

For eleven years, Sancia had honoured her father's wishes.

But a truth withheld is a tricky beast. It becomes a burden to the one who keeps it vaulted. It encumbers the soul, and can, in earnest, cause a sickness of the spirit to arise, with symptoms resembling a fever, even the dreaded pox.

Now, her body throttled with the chills, a conviction wrestled free from this secret load, like sunshine insisting its way through the clouds: Sancia wanted to live. To see her father again. To be pelted by questions she couldn't answer, yes, a rainfall of Teo's asking, as her mind brimmed and overflowed. Sancia was so tired of being afraid. She longed for the fear that tailed her to be banished once and for all. It had become a stalking shadow, a poisonous husk, impeding all joy. As long as she had Teo and her papa, what was there to fear?

'If I live,' she announced into the bleakness, 'if Papa and Teo return safely to me, I will never be afraid of anything again. This I vow.'

If a person makes a promise into empty space, bereft of a human listener, does it count?

Let us say it does, why not? For the chicken was there. It had been all along, trembling beneath the bed, equally bewildered and exiled from its own kin.

What chicken?

The one promised by the Marquis as a reward.

See, Gracia hadn't always been right.

On this windy night, stripped of its moon, Rodrigo stood at the old wooden door of Merdocai's home, wrapped in his hood and with a lantern in his hand.

He was, by recurrence, steeped in acquaintanceship with this threshold, which is exactly how he detected something awry. The step, you see, had been obscured with a nest of cistus leaves, lavender sprigs and birch twigs. If you knew, like Rodrigo did, that these were recent pluckings from the forest, since such flora did not grow anywhere in the village, perhaps you too would have knelt to scrabble in the foliage and in so doing, discover a small clay pot sealed with wax.

Before he even lifted it to his nose, he recognised what it was. A gift, rare and precious: honey.

But left under cover of the night, by whom?

Rodrigo knocked. 'T … Teo?'

He rested his ear on the door to listen for Isabel's snuffling, as she was wont to greet him thus whenever he would arrive. But not on this night. Much silence descended upon that stair. Rodrigo's heart beat faster, for there were too many curiosities and inconsistencies to settle this into the mundane.

He knocked again, this time more urgently. Did he hear moans? Surely not a squawk?

Against all pox-periled protocol, he turned the handle of the door. It creaked open.

The dwelling was blotted in blackness, without so much as a murmur from a dying ember in the hearth, which had been untended for hours. As he entered, he stumbled over a large obstruction at his feet. When he righted himself, he stood a moment to allow his eyes to accommodate the bleak light. In the far corner lay a body on the small wooden bed, atremble, too large for it to be Teo. Something alive pattered at his feet, too low, too light for it to be Isabel.

'Teo?' Sancia moaned. 'Is that you? I'm sorry … so sorry …'

Rodrigo wrapped his scarf around his mouth and nose and drew closer.

'Forgive me for sending you to Malakha,' Sancia wept. 'I did not know what else to do …'

These unwelcome words fell on Rodrigo's ears. Sancia had sent Teo to find Malakha? He rested the pot of honey and lantern on the small table. Light fell on the Marquis' pamphlet.

WILL YOU BE A HERO
TO END THE POX?

While some of us may be slow to piece together the baffling clues of a sack of wheat and a chicken in such irreconcilable circumstances, let us remember that Rodrigo was a thinker who perceived the thread that runs through all things, the glistening vein that loops through life. He understood that human existence was closer to the stars than the distance suggests. He felt the beat of the sap through the branches of trees as much as the rush of his own blood in his veins. There was, he knew, a secret artist at work, who laid things one over another, smitten with spirals and symmetry, and a design you had to half close your eyes to see clearly – echoes and repetitions we would come to know as fractals but which Rodrigo only saw as copies.

Without Sancia needing to speak another word, Rodrigo understood every part of what had transpired here. Each detail came together in his mind like pieces of a puzzle. A great pattern as intricate as that of the ferns of the forest and the constellations of the stars interlocked. In a moment, the full picture of what lay before him came into clear view.

A father who sacrifices himself for his children. A sister who sacrifices herself for her sister. There was only one word he knew for it – nothing he had ever encountered in his life so perfectly and exquisitely encompassed these circumstances: *tragedy*.

But at every turn, it was fuelled by love and selflessness. Every gesture was motivated by someone putting the one they loved before themself. Everything about it was mistaken and wrong, but there was nothing he could think of that was more beautiful and full of the frailties of misguided hope.

Right there, Rodrigo did what he had never done before.

He cried.

Chapter 18

In his chamber, the Marquis stroked the leather hood on Dante's sinking head.

All his authority was slipping through his fingers in the face of his goshawk's decline. Why, he could conquer villages, extract confessions from the innocent and, depending on the quality of his sleep, determine who might survive to eat their next meal or be denied tomorrow's dawn. Yet he could not instil wellbeing into the only creature whose life mattered to him. Something unbearable flared inside him. How could he be failing at this one small task? Where was his power to stop what was happening before his eyes?

His chest tightened. His ribs were shrinking around him, like claws closing in on prey. All of a sudden, he needed instructions on how to swallow, as if his throat had forgotten how to go about it.

'Torrero!' he thundered.

Graviel presented himself at the entrance to his chamber.

'How much longer must a marquis wait?'

Graviel floundered to muster a response. His hesitation drew the Marquis' fury.

'Where is the doctor? What conclusions has he drawn?'

Graviel blinked, casting his mind back over the days in which the doctor had refused to even examine Merdocai Beneviste, the Subject Matter. 'Surely he'd eat the slop and die? Only to be replaced by the next monkey?' was all the doctor had offered.

'He is ...'

The Marquis strained to co-ordinate the muscles in his mouth. He elevated his soft palate, closed off his nasal passages and contracted his pharynx so that he might gulp down the saliva that had pooled under his tongue to initiate the usually involuntary reflex of the autonomous nervous system.

Meanwhile, Graviel tried to imagine the conditions that present themselves to a man such that he would forsake his autonomy and give himself over to the vagaries of experimentation on the unscathed vessel of his body. He knew what hunger could do to a man. Once, in war, a starving soldier had hacked off the limb of a dead comrade, by the side of the road, and eaten it raw. By grace alone, Graviel had never fallen so far from what held him in place as a carnivore, not a cannibal, but he had peered over its precipice. He had seen a woman sell her own newborn, one no older than Beatris, for a loaf of stale bread. People were not inherently good or bad, it appeared, but circumstance converted them one way or the other.

'... there is no doubt ... he is ... poor, Muy Ilustre Señor Marqués.' It was the only adjective Graviel could grab on to. There were others he quickly dismissed as unsuitable to share with the Marquis. Words he couldn't quite find it in himself to speak out loud, but which slinked through the thicket of his pain like a deer stepping soundlessly into a forest clearing: *kind, noble, honourable.* Graviel bit down on his lips lest they slip out like flatulence one could hardly pin on another, given that it was just him and the Marquis in the chamber.

The Marquis felt the triggering of the swallowing reflex and downed his spittle ostentatiously. 'A Subject Matter is dispensable *because* he is poor.'

Dispensable was another four-syllable word, but Graviel needed no interpreter to understand its meaning.

'He does ... have ... a family. Two ... er ... children ...'

Sancia and Teodoro. He had memorised them. Graviel turned their names quietly inside his head, like two small bird's eggs in his palm. A name was a light. It glowed like a lamp in the window of a home you were always longing to make your way back to. Until they'd named her, Beatris was just a wish, as invisible as air, not even as graspable as a feather in the wind. Then the little body, a strange incomprehensible addition, another human, from the sum of Taresa plus Graviel. Then the name, Beatris, which in turn gave him a new name: Father.

'*Así que?*' the Marquis beckoned. 'So?'

'Well … it is the case, I imagine … he's not … dis-pen-sable to … to … to them.'

A vein on the side of the Marquis' head began to flicker. The monumental task of swallowing loomed ahead.

Graviel tried to picture his baby daughter looking into his face instead of the bloodshot eyes in front of him.

'What renders a man dispensable?' the Marquis propositioned.

'I wish to understand, Muy Ilustre Señor Marqués.'

The chamber stilled. Graviel did not budge his large head, but his eyes strayed involuntarily to the corner, where the sight of the bird's bowed head covered in the imperial leather hood thrust an unspeakable desolation through him.

'When. I. Say. So.' The Marquis' voice was hoarse and harsh.

Perhaps there are no orchestrations as improbable

and numinous as those that arise spontaneously, without human curation. For at this juncture, another of Dante's feathers plummeted to the floor. It was almost soundless.

The Marquis' heart pounded like an army of witch-hunting soldiers closing in for slaughter. Dante was not just a common goshawk. No-one understood. He was anything but dispensable.

'At my command!' the Marquis howled.

'At your command, Muy Ilustre Señor Marqués,' Graviel repeated.

One would need to have been in the chamber alongside these men to vouch for an unadulterated retelling, but Graviel's parroting of the Marquis' insistence, an apparent imitation, exposed an uncommon tone for the status of his subservience. Perhaps it was the panic in the Marquis' eyes that caused some long-awaited understanding to land in him. Graviel's words were not recited in deference or by rote, but in the pitch of one man consoling another.

For all the wealth and power the Marquis had accumulated, he had never gathered any soft materials from which to sow the fields of his life. That is why he built spires instead of archways, chose unforgiving granite over the tenderness of moss, erected walls instead of bridges, meted out punishment instead of honours.

Graviel finally knew something the Marquis did not.
And you are about to know it too.
The Marquis did not know better.
He did not know.

Chapter 19

In his cell, Merdocai Beneviste finally surrendered. He abandoned his calls for help. A man comes to learn when he has lost everything, even the harsh conditions of an unremarkable life. Beyond the scolding and chastisement for his own gullibility and stupidity, he arrived at a tentative newfound threshold of perception.

In this state, he closed his eyes, and before him appeared the dear faces of his children – Sancia with her dark hair and smokey eyes, and Teo with her copper tufts and singularly astute eye. These merged in his mind until the clear and perfect vision of his wife, Gracia de Luna, rose in front of him. It comforted him to see her face once again.

She had been the triumph of his life. The only reward a man could hope for – to be seen by another, to be loved, with all his shortcomings and failures, of which there were many, beginning with the two fingers he'd lost on a winch, pulling in a catch of fish. She had adored him despite the scars he'd brought home from the Great War. She had chosen him, above all others, a humble fisherman.

He envisioned her now, his Gracia, as the young woman he'd first laid eyes on, mother-at-last to Sancia, wise and womb-weary; how she used to brush her hair by candlelight, a ritual of untangling and unknotting. If he had to say what sight he missed most, it came to just this – the slender curve of her spine, the tilting of her neck, the combing of her locks and her face half in shadow, innocent of her own radiance.

But something else happened as he deepened into the memory, something he had never noticed before: was that a small frown on Gracia's brow? He crept closer to the vision to fully apprehend what seemed to be gathering there. Though it was not easy for a husband to observe, it was as clear as anything, her stifled unruliness. In this veiled hallway of half-hauntings, he wondered with shame if his love had been a jess, a restraint on the untameable nature that raged inside her, as unpredictable and maddening as the ocean's. He had never, you must believe, meant to domesticate her; only to keep her safe. It is an oft-recited notion that one cannot love too much, but that is only true if one can bear to lose who and what one loves, without the precaution of locking them away for safekeeping. Merdocai wept as he finally grasped that she had never belonged to him, but to something so much larger.

She had always seemed to Merdocai to be a woman on the edge of life. Being with her, he sensed he could lose her at any moment. This feeling became stronger as time went by, and they couldn't have a child. A gradual foreboding welled up in him. Each time he returned home to find her there, at the stove, he would meet her as if for the first time.

With every fallen pregnancy, something wilder took hold of her, a rashness he feared would cause her to overreach. After Sancia arrived, something settled in her for a time. Then, when she miraculously fell pregnant, life was blessed and she was his, and they were a family.

But nothing was the same after the day she lost the little thing, when it was so close, she could almost nurse it.

Now he recalled how once she had lain in his arms and had turned to him with a faraway look that terrified him.

'If it should happen that I die young …'

'Why do you taunt me?' He kissed the top of her head.

Gracia pulled away. 'We must speak of important things. Even those that scare us …'

He did not argue with her – though, looking back, he often wished he had pulled her from the brink.

Perhaps if he had dispossessed her of such speakings, she might not have taken such risks.

She had curled her hand into his. 'If I die before you, I will come back …'

'To haunt me?'

'… to tell you what lies beyond …'

'I wish for you to stay right here with me. Can you promise me?'

She had arranged herself to rest her head on her bent arm, and held him with her gaze.

'I cannot promise …'

Merdocai sighed. 'Why not try, my love?'

She shook her head. 'If I should leave this life first, I will return with a sign.'

When she talked of dreams and signs, he felt the future bearing down on them both. The only way to restrain it, to redirect it, was with humour.

'Will you come back as fish or fowl?' he teased. 'An enormous bream? Perhaps an albatross around my neck? How will I know it's you, and not mistake you for my dinner?'

But she did not laugh, nor take the joke further, as was her way. Her brow furrowed, as it did when she was drawing down a thought.

'I will return … as a duckling.'

Merdocai laughed. 'Not even a fully grown duck?'

A tiny smile flickered on her lips, as if she was

willing at last to step with him into the lightness. 'That way, you will at least have to wait for me to grow big enough to fill your belly.'

All anecdotes are angled by the meaning ascribed in the aftermath and so, by Merdocai's retelling, this became a story about how the ocean had brought them together.

Before life had brought their paths to cross, he had seen, over many seasons, a solitary figure roaming on the rocks. Each day, as he brought in his fishing vessel, his eyes wandered to the woman chiselling oysters and mussels in the distance. He had only ever seen her from afar, but what an otherworldly notion, to feel as if he knew her already. It was told, amongst those who chattered about such things, that she harvested the biggest and juiciest oysters, to stoke any libido – for it was said that the power of lust and passion nestled in the salty quiver of an oyster. Even the thought of her made Merdocai blush.

One autumn neap tide, when the variance between high and low tides was barely detectable, Merdocai dragged in his nets, retrieving a moderate haul of sardines but not a single bream. Within the catch was nestled a peculiar metal object with two pronged tines. A tool such as this, he knew, was used only by royalty – for eating, of all activities, as if a knife and spoon and two hands were inadequate. Perhaps it had been tossed overboard by a royal ship beyond the horizon, or was the singular remnant of a shipwreck, a merchant haul interrupted by pirates. Grasping this improbable thing in his hands, he knew its purpose. It had a rightful owner.

The noon sun blinded him at first, but out there she was, bent over, hard at work. Clutching the fork in his hands and before his thinking intervened to interrupt his instinct, he strode across the beach towards the rocks.

The boulders of the crag were challenging and demanded strong thighs, sure feet and a single-minded purpose. The heat bore down on him, drenching him in sweat, weakening his prospects of the kind of first impression a man dreams of making. Just as he doubted whether this was indeed a good plan, as right as anyone might conceive on impulse, she appeared in front of him, startled and startling him. She too was soaked in sweat, her face streaked with salt and sun. Her hands were bloodied and blistered from her labour. His shyness might have overtaken him. Still, he held out the fork.

Puzzled for a moment, she paused, and then she reached her hand to accept this perfect gift, her smile billowing over him like a net.

From then on, with every tide that came and went the emptiness inside each of them became filled with the other. How long did it take before Merdocai loved her and before she loved him? How long is a fork?

The lingering wait of years before they met dissolved, and time sped up. Oaths were uttered about forever, rings made of brass were exchanged. Merdocai awoke each morning, roused and invigorated to take in the tangle of Gracia's hair on the pillow beside him. Curling a finger through her ringlets, he swore that a man might wait his whole life just for the pleasure of a woman's hair wrapped around his pointer digit.

As soon as she awoke, she'd tumble into telling him her dreams – how she flew through deep water and swirled with eagles. Often, dark visions came to her while she slept – of the air turning poisonous, the seas rising to swallow villages and the last whale dying.

It was never his intention to stifle her, but Merdocai begged her not to mention her dreams to anyone but him. 'You know what they will do if your visions come to pass.'

'I am not afraid of them,' she reminded him.

Armed with her fork, she became more daring in her exploration of the aeolian promontory that jutted far into the bay. Lashed by waves and currents for as long as rock has met water, it was no timid task to traverse, especially when the tide came in. Timing is often overlooked as a safeguard to action, but there are instances where it is all that matters. Gracia assured Merdocai that she always watched the moon's waxing and waning, and waited for the perfect minutes in the perfect hours to harvest the richest and creamiest oysters for a stew spiked with all the tanginess of the ocean.

And life would have continued this way if that had been life's plan. Alas, these short years were a brief gift, from which the sands of time were running from the moment Merdocai handed Gracia the ocean fork.

Merdocai didn't see it. No-one who spoke and retold the tale of it had.

Some whispered it had been a freak wave. A king tide. A wall, a tower of water. An accident. When hearsayers told the story of that day, they spoke of the crash and gulp and gasp as she was engulfed, the fork spinning from her hand, the suck and swirl of the surf off the rocks. These were tales rich with the elaborations and embellishments of ones who had never perceived what they claimed to have seen with their own binocular-visioned eyes, for this is how stories come to be.

Merdocai had played these accounts in his mind over and over.

He had rowed his boat across every inch of the bay to find her. Calling and crying and crying and calling.

But the sea, one discovers in a terrible hour, is indifferent, and the same wherever you turn. It does not mean to elude or deceive, but when something is gone beneath its lilting waves, it is, I am sorry to say, gone forever.

When he finally wrenched his boat to shore in the gloaming, after every shred of the day's light had withered, his lips were chapped and bleeding from the salt and the sun. He was emptied of all hope and broken by the sea. He was no longer the man he had been that very same morning as he kissed Gracia goodbye and promised to bring home the biggest bream he could catch.

Sunken to the sand on his shins, his heart in shreds, he bellowed.

It was then that a figure stepped out from who-knows-where and kneeled beside him.

'Save your tears,' she instructed.

'For what and for whom?' he whimpered. 'All is lost. Life is over.'

The crash of the waves as they shattered shoreward hissed as they had always done and would always do. There was no way of seeing distinctly in that shrinking light, especially as the gloom of grief had swindled this man of his spirit. Though she might have been an apparition, the sound of a baby's cry roused him.

Shaken from his trance, he strained to try and see what was in front of his eyes. An old woman. A skep washed up on the beach. A baby in her arms, drenched to the bone. Gracia's fork in her hand.

'It wasn't breathing when I found it,' she said. She handed him the sodden bundle. 'This is what she drowned for.'

'What will I do with it?' he sobbed.

'What she would have,' La Primera de los Ojos said.

Chapter 20

It has been a stretch since we were last with Teo, but time, as we know, is both mercurial and relative; it flows and is stationary all at once, depending on its chronological or kairotic temperament. While we have been detouring its labyrinthine passages, Teo has all this while been seated beside the old woman, who – when last we encountered her – had pulled back a curtain on her hidden history. Perhaps this is what is meant when we say, 'Time stood still.' There was much that Teo needed to feel and ponder before she was able to ask her next question.

'You *saved* me? From what?'

The old woman brought a small piece of kindling, a splinter of wood, to her mouth, as if to dislodge an encumbrance from between her teeth. For all we know, this dental interruption might have been a contrivance to slacken the momentum of revelation, which is a lesser-known kindness exhibited by those who grasp the limitations of the human heart for absorbing more than it can take.

Teo's head was swirling with noisy questions, but the old woman made her wait until she did indeed extricate a splinter of cinnamon bark from between her teeth.

'I wasn't the first or the only one. She tried. Oh, she did. Threw herself into the waves, all to bring you home.'

What was the old woman speaking of?

'I don't understand …'

'Remember …'

'What must I remember?'

'Your dream.'

Teo reared back in amazement.

'How … how do you know about my dream?'

'It is right here with us. You are carrying it, are you not? We dream so as not to forget. How else do we keep things from getting lost?'

Teo could not deny that the dream was always in her head, on her tongue, in the round-abouts of her person. She squeezed her eye shut and reeled the dream in from its fathoms.

'I am wrapped in a blanket of water.'

'Because you were.'

'I am crying for my mother.'

'Oh, I heard those cries.'

'I swallowed saltwater.'

'There was a small leak,' the old woman nodded.

'I started breathing the sea.'

'You were almost lost. If not for the whale.'

Teo's whole body felt alive, as if stung with a million tiny pricks of something sharp and hot. Abuzz.

'Tell me about the whale,' she begged.

'It is not for me to say why the whale was there, but I saw it with my own two once-I-had-them eyes.'

'What did the whale do?'

'Only you can remember.'

Teo placed her hands over her eye sockets. The warmth of her palms steadied and soothed her. She tried to fall backwards into her dream, to bring it into her deeper eye. 'It ... sang to me.'

'*Sí, es cierto*,' the old woman clucked. 'It pushed the basket almost to shore. It nearly beached itself in the effort, and what a sacrifice that would have been.'

A deep tenderness rose inside Teo as she felt the echoed nudge of the whale's body against the skep, the clanks and spackling squeaks of the whale's song as it bumped her back to shore. It was as if the memory was living inside her blood, a river that connected her to the whale, the way all waterways are connected to the ocean.

'The whale saved me ... and so did you.'

'Now you're remembering.' The old woman sighed.

The fire flared as the wind began to pick up. The forest rattled and whipped around them. Teo wrapped her cape tightly around her. The old woman, draped in her pine marten and rabbit fur shawl, seemed unchanged by the weather.

La Primera de los Ojos lifted her hands as if she were tracing the shape of something unseen.

'Gota Fría is coming,' she mumbled. 'And with it, Malakha will trail. She loves a storm.'

'How will I find Her, Doña?' Teo asked, reminded of why she was here.

'It is not for you to find Her. Malakha does the finding. But I will be visiting Her soon.' The old woman nodded. 'Give me your fork so I may pass it on to Her.'

Teo paused. How could she part with the only object in her possession which might be swapped for a miracle? She felt the night's wind on her cheeks.

Without her fork, she would certainly be travelling empty-handed. But the old woman knew where Malakha was and she did not. What choices were left

to her?

'It is right to wonder whether you can trust me,' the old woman said, as if she were able to see inside Teo's head.

Teo caressed the metal object in her fingers, for the last time, before passing it into the ancient hands. They clasped it close. The old woman seemed satisfied, as if she had been waiting for it a long time. With her fingertips, she tested the tines and stroked the mother-of-pearl handle.

'Malakha only devours – She does not resurrect. She does not hold the cure for your sister.'

Teo wished the old woman had shared this revelation before she'd handed over her precious fork. But it was too late now.

'Where will I find a cure then?' Teo asked, unbidden tears welling up inside her.

'Perhaps a cure is not yours to find.'

'But I have been sent to find one,' Teo wept.

At the sound of her tears, Isabel lifted her head. With her duckling-bonnet, she rose to her feet, trotted

over to Teo and laid her head in Teo's lap. Teo fondled her ears and, with her forefinger, petted Patito.

The old woman's voice was gentle now. 'What if you came all this way to give me this fork?'

'I do not understand. How will it help save Sancia? I cannot lose my sister.'

'Lose her? Is she a fork, or an eye? You are carrying her inside you, like you carry your dream. All cures come in their time, some from inside us, and some from' – the old woman gestured with her hands to the sky, lifting her wooden staff and pointing to the treetops that canopied them – 'everywhere.'

Suddenly the unbearable separation from the one object that tied her to her history overtook Teo. 'You will give Malakha my mother's fork and beg Her for a miracle?'

'She' – the old woman paused as she fingered the tines – 'was not your only mother.'

'She was, I believe.'

'Don't believe everything you believe.'

Teo was confounded, like she often was when Rodrigo spoke in riddles, but a small ire flickered now. What could one trust in, if not one's beliefs?

'Does not every child come from one mother?' Teo asked, her heart bouncing in her chest. 'Even Isabel had a mother, Esmeralda, a less friendly goat than she. And Patito has a mother too, even if she has lost her.'

'What do you see?' the old woman asked, gesturing to their forested surroundings. Teo turned her head this way and that, and took in all her eye could drink. The brown earth beneath her feet. The sheltering elms and oaks towering above them and the hidden shadows behind them. The branches draped in swathes of Spanish moss, the bespeckled rocks, pebbles, lichen and gravel.

'Listen …' The old woman paused.

The fire beside them ticked and snapped. A million creatures in the forest crept and crawled, called and caressed, hunted and howled.

'All this,' she said, 'mothers you.'

The fire popped.

Somewhere in the forest, an owl whooped.

Isabel snuffled sleepily.

'But there must have been one who birthed me. If not Gracia de Luna, then whom?' Teo asked.

'At last it is time, child. I have waited a long while to tell you the story of where you came from.'

Chapter 21

Before we eavesdrop on the old woman's revelations, let us turn our attention back to the small, dark cabin in the village where Rodrigo stands at the foot of Sancia's bed, thirteen years of unshed tears streaming from his eyes.

Imagine if you had saved every sorrow and buried each one in a safe place for a 'someday'; what a treasure would await when at long last you returned to reclaim it. Rodrigo felt the gush, the rush, the plush pulsing, as if he'd struck a vein in the secret water tables of the earth.

His heart cracked like the ground after an earthquake, and the tremors of it loosened a cradle song inside him he had forgotten. It must have been hummed into him when he was just a precious babysweet boy, and his mother, Josefa, had rocked his head in the crook of her soft, strong arms and rested her lips on his newborn brow.

It came to him, as if he had never lost it or put it down anywhere, but had been carrying it all along in a hidden pouch of his being. The words had been lost in the haze of unremembered times, but the melody left his mouth clear and strong.

As he sang in the lessening darkness, Rodrigo rekindled the fire using the flame of his lantern. The hen clucked appreciatively and waddled from under the bed to be closer to the warmth. There, on a tuft of straw, sat a single perfect egg. Perhaps it was the sight of this ovoid wonder, a layer of calcium carbonate enclosing membranes, clear albumen and a perfect orange yolk, that unleashed a knowing seeded inside him, sourced from his long-gone mother's baking hands. Some things are passed on by the instruction of kinfolk, like *one, two* and the acceptable orientations of a B or a P. But others are woven through us, echoes of our originators, in the tiny records of ancestry we now call genes. It is, without exaggeration, a miraculous epigenetic finding that we carry silent memories, perhaps even those belonging to ones who came before us.

Otherwise, how would Rodrigo have known what to do next?

With his knife, he pried open the pot of honey left in stealth by enigmatic means. Everyone knew that the body pleads for the healing in the golden nectar bees pass from one to another. In these times, people clashed, even dare we mention, *killed*, for honey, a sacred ingredient in anti-pox medicines. Someone had risked their safety to place it here, and had forgone its treasure for themselves.

Who would sacrifice such sustenance in these times? Unbeknownst to Rodrigo, Sancia, or even less likely, Teo – only a mother.

He withdrew his knife from his belt, made a small incision in the sack of wheat and scooped two handfuls into a brass pot. He crumbled cinnamon bark from his scrip, before adding water, a dollop of honey and a pinch of fermenting starter from the leaven pot on the windowsill. He held the warm egg in his hands and, with utmost care not to lose a single drop of its minerals, fats and proteins, he cracked it into the mixture. With his rough hands, he churned the elements into dough, and when it was blended he set it over the fireplace.

'Where is she?' Sancia called out.

'Shh ... eee is ... safe,' Rodrigo comforted.

'Where is Papa?' she gasped.

'He ... eee is alm-m-m ... os-s-st h-hom-me.'

'Where is my mama?'

'Sheee is r-r-right-t h-heee ... re b-be ... s-side youuu ...'

And so, as the fire conversed with the dough, and the baking proceeded, Rodrigo stuttered assurances and quelled Sancia's tremors, no matter how often she called out. Soon, the smell of a honey cake filled the room.

In the droning fog of her fever, in which hours, days and minutes blended into timelessness, Sancia smelled light around her. She breathed it in.

The surging contagion tried to pull her back. But the aroma of honey and cinnamon wrestled her from its grip. Her head thrashed from side to side, as nasal passages lined with sensory receptors sent private notes to her brain for interpretation. Thus the olfactory cortex and limbic system of her brain awoke, triggering memories and emotions.

Long before fear had owned her, Sancia had belonged to a home held in place with a mother and a father and Tía Clara and excursions to the ocean each day. Potatoes were potatoes then, and pebbles just pebbles. *Uno, dos*, one, two ... The seagulls had called with friendly summons overhead. Imperial eagles had crossed the sky, on their way back to their families, and her mama pointed at them and her papa tossed her high into the air to reach them. She'd run back and forth across the sand, trying to place her footprints inside the larger ones of her mama. Back home, her mama baked strawberry breads and corn dumplings in broth.

As the smell of honey filled the room, now warm and alive with Rodrigo's humming and the clucking of a chicken, Sancia began to remember it all, and the past returned to her in all its goodness.

When the baking was complete, Rodrigo set the pot on the table and cut a warm slice with his knife. He kneeled at her bedside, and, crumb by crumb, he fed it into Sancia's open mouth, spooning it in with sips of water to aid her swallowing. Like a baby bird, she yielded.

He then wrapped a cool cloth around her brow and tucked a blanket around her to coax the fever out.

When she finally fell asleep, the heat from her body slowly receding, Rodrigo cut two more slices of the cake and slipped them into his scrip, before he let himself out and made his way back to the forest to find Teo.

A storm was coming. And she was out looking for Malakha.

There are some questions every heart needs the answers to. Who am I? Where did I come from? Why am I here? But there is a smaller one that requires only one word to meet it – one name, to be precise: who will come looking for me when I go missing?

Chapter 22

When Shems stumbled through the front door to a darkened shack, without candlelight or a blaze-filled hearth, he did not fret for Rodrigo's safety. It was not in his nature to tarry in the quicksands of worry. His worst fears had come to pass when he'd lost Josefa, and since then he had turned his back against hurts-that-had-not-yet-happened. He knew that when disaster struck – as it would in every life, no matter how seemingly blessed – a man would have to be ready to bear its blows. Nothing could prepare him for the shock or the agony. Until then, the only honest way he knew was to keep shovelling earth over bodies and not further burden his fatigue by imagining what may or may not be.

Rodrigo's explorations of the forest, which sometimes kept him for days, were a growing boy's way of finding his place in the world. Shems understood that he did not understand the love Rodrigo had for the woods, the way it was impossible for anyone to appreciate Shems' devotion to Josefa. He did not question or trouble his son for explanations.

To be smitten was a private matter.

To observe any love from afar is a runoff of joy, in which the onlooker is touched by the overflow. Shems simply bowed his head in thanks whenever Rodrigo came back from his woodland meanderings, eyes bright with new encounters, his scrip and pouch bursting with roots and shoots and his mouth stuttering with poems.

On this night, after laying so many bodies to rest in one short day, Shems' exhaustion overtook him. He fell onto his cot, unfed and unwarmed, into the pit of sleep.

Shems dreamed of bread. Through the hours of the dark-gloved night, he dreamed of sheaves of wheat. Behind his eyelids, he conjured up clouds of soft white flour, light as a rainbow, billowy and wafting – not the coarse barley, oats and buckwheat of the poor bread he and Rodrigo ate when they could get hold of it.

The bread in his dreaming head did not need to be soaked in soup to be edible, like the trencher, which was hard and flat and especially gruelling for one without canines or incisors. His dreaming bread was as puffy and pale as a dove's underbelly.

In his dream – which permits all delights, no matter how far-fetched and out of reach they may be upon waking – he sinks his hands far into the yielding, ale-doused dough. It is milky and velvety, not as dark as soil. It sticks to his fingers, a viscous adhesion which smells richly of the gurgling swirl of living yeast. He kneads for the sake of things to rise, instead of digging to lower bodies into the ground. He is baking breads to fill bellies. Not shovelling earth to fill graves.

Shems dreams of hunger, his own and others, satiated by the smallest motion of a hand dipping a piping hot slice of bread in a bowl of broth, and the comfort it surely brings, so that every mouth might suck on the tender chewy folds and know that all is as it should be in the world.

It is not an exaggeration to say that Shems, even in his sleep, was smitten with bread.

The first time he'd seen Josefa, it was barely daybreak. He had almost bumped into her as she'd charged out of the king's bakery, carrying a tray of piping hot bread.

'*Perdón*, I'm sorry,' she gasped.

Her cheeks were pinked from the heat of the ovens and her bodice was stained with sweat. Her sleeves were rolled up, and her arms were as strong as any man's he had ever seen. Bakers worked long and strange hours, getting up in the middle of the night to bake bread fresh for the Marquis' breakfast. By the time the sun came up, most of their workday was over, and it was time to start fixing for the next day's bake.

Shems tried to speak, to let her know that she had nothing to be sorry for. No, in fact, he was the one who should have taken more care, not to walk so … straight. He was mortified not to have anticipated that a busy baker might be barging out from the bakery when the light was still so subdued, and could he help her with her heavy load?

Perhaps it was the slant of dawn's first light on her warm face, mingled with the smell of freshly baked loaves and the endearing smear of flour across her cheek, like a dusting of snow on his window frame, that caused Shems' tongue to stick to the roof of his mouth as if it had been nailed there. Where was his speech? It had evaporated like the sails of night as the sunlight poured like blond honey all around her in a moment in which all his senses frothed and bubbled.

She strode on, almost running up the street towards the citadel, her skirt fluttering behind her. In his head, he imagined he knew her name and saw himself calling it out after her; in this vision, upon hearing it she turned and smiled. Just the fiction of this was enough for a man to understand that his life would never be the same again.

Shems carried a lute in his arms, light as a shell of bark. His father had chopped the tree from which it was made, and he'd watched him build it over many months, bending the wood and fixing it before he produced the final instrument and played it with his nimble fingers.

Shems parted with the lute at the door of the king's winery, in return for a lump of natural yeast and a sack of flour. He had cared for that lute, which brought his father's voice back with every string plucked. But Shems did not make his home in the past. He knew that no soul could travel to the next world carrying a single item from his life, not even one he had made by hand.

All he could hold was the tenderness in his spirit.

And so he traded the lute for the prospect of finding a way to Josefa's love.

Is it a solace to know that he had never, not once, regretted the exchange?

Chapter 23

Back in the forest, in the wake of a more recent exchange, La Primera de los Ojos shuffled on the tree stump on which she sat.

Reams of Spanish moss with which the forest was adorned offered ample cushioning for younger sitting bones, but her frame – timeworn over many dark years and readying for a long and final rest – ached. She bent forward to feel for her brass bowl and took a long slug of her forest soup. *Ahhhh.*

It had been too many turns of the sun since she had been graced with the vibrance of a child's company, and it filled her with a formidable and shepherding yearning. She licked her lips and wiped her mouth with the back of her hand. A soup sipped in companionship was altogether a different soup than one slurped alone. Flavours altered in the humidities of hospitality.

'Tell me, Doña, who was she?' the child repeated, as if it might have slipped through the slats of the old woman's remembering that a mothering story had been called in around this fire.

The old woman cleared her throat. 'We must, of course, begin with a bulrush.'

Teo waited. A bulrush? A bulrush? Yes?

'Well, do you not wish to know why?'

'Yes, yes, Doña,' the child implored. 'Why a bulrush?'

'Once, back then' – she indicated over her shoulder – 'in the loops of the past, the mother of a young child swaddled him in a basket and set the basket amongst the bulrushes. She sent it down the river for, then, to be a boy was a dangerous state of affairs ...'

'I do know this story,' Teo murmured. 'Papa has told it many times.'

'Let us keep this tale in mind, shall we,' the old woman continued.

A long, untampered silence arose. The child waited wonderingly inside it as the teller gathered up the broken pieces of history to lay them out in front of her.

'Sometimes, a woman cannot bear her own children,' the old woman went on. 'It is not caused by wickedness or fault. It happens.'

'Why is that so?'

La Primera de los Ojos shrugged. 'It is sometimes the way of Nature to be ... otherwise. Gracia de Luna, who fell in love by this fork, was one such woman.'

'You knew my mother?' The child was ablaze with puzzlement.

'I knew Gracia de Luna. I also knew your mother.'

'But …?'

The old woman held up her hands. 'It is not a riddle. Let us tell more.'

Teo sighed and fidgeted.

'And sometimes those who can bear children are unable to bear the responsibility of such a precious life. But not … for lack of love.'

The old woman took another slurp of her soup, as if to allow the child a moment to grasp what she had just imparted.

'This brings me to your fluffy friend, the merganser.'

Teo looked down at Patito, who was fast asleep on Isabel's head.

'Where, we might ask, is the mother duck?'

Teo shrugged. 'If only we could ask Isabel, for she is the one who found her.'

'Leave the goat to her slumber. I'll tell you where. The mother is gone. She laid her egg in the nest of another bird so that it might raise her young. For such is the way of a merganser mother. Not good, not bad. It is a ducking sort of a duck.'

'I see …' Teo murmured.

'You will, in time.'

Teo ran her finger over the little duckling's head. 'Poor Patito.'

'Mergansers are not the most clucky of creatures. But why make this a failing when they are resourceful? A woman, too, may give birth to a daughter in grim times. Perhaps she fears for her own life, for we are all born into injustices and miseries not of our creation. And so … what if she were to cast her child into the waters, hoping to save it – as an act of great love?'

Teo gathered every word that fell from the old woman's mouth like foraged berries. *Bulrush. Merganser. Childless mother. Mother who cast her child upon the waters.* A peculiar feeling began to climb inside her. Why were all these legends coming to claim her? And what did love have to do with it?

'Such a child, perhaps swaddled in a woven skep, a beehive lined with wax, cast out upon the sea, might be spotted by a damsel with a fork, collecting oysters on the rocks.'

Teo's heart rattled so loudly in her ears she could barely hear the words that followed.

'Such a fearless one might throw herself into the waves, to try and rescue that child.'

'To save her from drowning?' Teo murmured.

'But perhaps the waters were too strong.'

Teo's dream began to rise. A basket, the ocean, swallowing the water.

'And another by chance might have witnessed this act of bravery and managed to save the baby, but not the woman.'

Suddenly, a stream of sensation flooded Teo.

A memory. That is what Rodrigo had said.

Rodrigo's words were broken and slow, but they were always the truth.

Out in the pelagic slosh and heave, the blue whale felt a pull towards the bay of his birth. Over vast tracts of open ocean with seemingly no identifiable features, far from all landmarks, he had traversed, using, it is surmised, the earth's magnetic field to navigate, or even perhaps the position of the sun and the moon to guide him. Even today, it is still not known, only conjectured, how he and all his whale counterparts are able to steer a course so precise and straight over such unimaginable distances as to confound scientists. It is a poetics of causation that would have thrilled Teo and Rodrigo, and is surely still one of the great unsolved mysteries of the world.

Eleven years, three months and seventeen days in the past, for those who are counting time in this way, this very blue whale had returned to the bay of Dazic.

As he breached for breath, his right eye had caught sight of a human figure on the cliffs, throwing itself into the waves. In the few seconds in which his body thrust upwards and skywards, his ears had caught a piercing sound unlike any he had ever heard before. Cascading back into the depths, he'd swung the ship of his body towards a human cry that came from a basket bobbing on the surface of the sea, which he had taken in with his left eye.

A whale has no human sense of time, from what we can tell, so perhaps to him it was all part of one endless moment, as he found himself coursing in vast circles through the water, singing to Gracia's lifeless body. To him, she was as much a part of the landscape of this homecoming bay as the bluffs and the winds. We cannot determine how whales grieve, but perhaps we can surmise that they know how to depart this life well when left to die on their own terms.

Though Gracia could no longer hear, his whoops and twitters were heard long and deep and far away by other whales travelling towards their next great feed.

He touched her body with the great hulk of his head, before rising to the surface to nudge a floating basket filled with a baby's cries towards the shore.

A stranger on a cliff had died trying to save her. The immensity of it all struck Teo in the heart. Tears could not help themselves from seeping from her eyes. Was she to blame for Gracia's death? Gracia … the mother of her sister, Sancia, but not her own. Was Sancia no longer her sibling? A riot of upending questions scrambled inside her, what-ifs and whys and hows in a havoc that rendered her momentarily voiceless.

When Teo spoke, she tried to hold the tremble in her voice. 'Who was she? My real mother?'

The old woman hesitated.

'Tell me, please. I want to know. What was her name? And what was the sound of her voice? And the colour of her eyes?'

'Valentina.'

'Valentina,' Teodoro said. 'Valentina. Valentina.'

'A beekeeper.'

'A keeper of bees?' Teo shivered to hold this new intelligence.

It seemed to Teo that the old woman knew all there was to know. As if she had a key to all the locked vaults of not only her own small life, but all life. How insignificant she felt.

Imagine, nestled in the securities of our own kinship bonds, the shock to a young person in discovering her history by these circumventing means. Conceive, if you can, the cacophony of such calamitous revelations on the heart and mind of Teo as she thumped against the notion that her stories did not even belong to her, and as those to which she held herself in belonging crumbled mendaciously to dust.

Let us abide a while, as many a confoundment hangs there in the forest on this night.

When at last the ground steadied beneath her, Teo found the strength for one final and courageous clarification.

'You said my father was a liar.' Teo's voice broke as she spoke.

'I would never lie about a lie.'

'How did I lose my eye if not for a fishhook?'

The old woman scratched her nose. 'Well, what is the one thing you fear? And do not say nothing, for there is one.'

'… I do not …' Teo paused. '… Bees, I am afraid of bees.'

'*Absolutamente*. One lone one. Trapped in the skep. A sting most unfortunate, on a delicate eyeball, for which the bee paid with its life. But there was nothing to be done. If I hadn't removed it, you might have lost both eyes. Then what a pair you and I would make. The blind leading the blind.' She chuckled darkly.

Teo lifted the patch of cloth covering the empty socket of her eye, to feel the small aperture that connected her to the old woman, her mother and the whale.

'You … took my eye?'

'All things arrive full of possibilities, in the right hands, at the right time,' the old woman said, holding up the fork.

'With my mother's fork?'

'She left it behind, wedged in the rocks. Besides, she had no use for it, at the bottom of the ocean.'

By the light of the fire, the tines of the fork glinted.

There comes a moment in every life when we must let go, not only of the stories we carry, but the things that hold us to them. Teo, make no mistake, is in this moment riven with both grief and gratitude. But given a little more time, she will be both lightened and enlightened by the parting from that ill-fated fork.

We must leave Teo and the old woman now, while the storm gathers out at sea and exhaustion pulls Teo into a deep and dreamless sleep.

And if the light does not dupe us, perhaps it is long-awaited rapture on the face of La Primera de los Ojos, as she aims a fork towards some blind heaven.

Chapter 24

The Marquis stood at the window of his chamber, surveying the citadel. Where was the moon this night? He craned his neck, but the clouds had locked elbows in a battalion of impenetrable cumulonimbus. From afar, the winds were gathering, coming in from the sea. He willed the storm to disperse, for winds and wild weather agitated him.

He remembered his mother on nights when the moon was eclipsed, and no light found its way through the sky. Such skies always made Lazaro de Abismo feel particularly melancholy, and a vast loneliness rose in him.

He'd once had a father, a grim wolf of a man with a beard and remote eyes, whose perversions spurred him to hurt small creatures until they cowered, in the silent ways animals know how to plead for mercy. As a young boy, he had amassed many thrashings from his father, the last time being when he, through innocent carelessness, brought mud indoors on the soles of his bare feet. Not long after, his father disappeared. His mother, Inez, had told him that his father had been eaten by a wild bear in the forest.

'Though he likely took one bite and spat him out, for even bears cannot eat only bile and bitterness,' she quipped.

On dim-lit nights during the most egregious anguishes of the famine, when she believed her son fast asleep, Inez would slip out the front door of the cramped quarters they called their home, and be gone without a word, leaving him all alone till the early hours.

Little Luciano would stand at the window, leaning on his strong leg, and wait for her to return to dispel his abandonment during nights when even the moon did not offer an illuminated respite from desperation. Sometimes he'd wake with a jolt when he slipped to the floor, having fallen asleep on his feet. In the mornings he'd ask her, 'Mama, where did you go last night?'

'I was here the whole time.'

But how then were her shoes dirtied? Where had the wild garlic, mushrooms, roots and berries come from to fill his aching belly? Sometimes there was even a vole or two his mother skinned and turned into stew.

Still, she insisted, 'You must have been dreaming, Luciano.'

Then he would wonder whether he was mistaken, for mothers were truthful, or else what sense was there in the world?

Then came the day the King's soldiers arrived. Luciano saw their boots from beneath the bed where he often hid from his father.

They dragged his mother out of their home by her long, brown hair.

'Inez, the Witch!' the neighbours chanted, and though Luciano was ignorant of such hypocrisies, they were, it is distressing to divulge, the very ones who sidled to her front door under cover of night to swap clothing, blankets or the occasional shank of a boar for the potions she brewed whenever the moon grew dark.

The soldiers smashed her bottles of tinctures and torched their home. Luciano coughed and spluttered as he crawled through the flames. When he emerged, his mother was chained to a horse, being dragged in the dirt. He ran on his crippled leg behind them, until they stopped at the river.

'Swim the Witch,' the villagers sang, the very ones who ventured in secret to show Inez their rashes, heartaches and misfortunes, for which they grasped the herbs and oils she pressed into their palms.

In the long grass, Luciano cried for his mama as the soldiers stripped her down to her underclothes and tied her right big toe to her left hand and her left big toe to her right hand. So knotted, they threw her into the water.

'If she sinks, she is innocent. If she floats, she is a witch,' the villagers hissed, the very ones who by stealth kept returning for their vessels to be refilled when their remedies for fertility, forlornness or fever ran low.

'Sink, Mama, sink,' he cried, but his voice was trapped in his throat.

Alas, Luciano's mother floated.

Inez knew what was at stake. She ducked her head under the water. She tried to turn upside down. But she kept bobbing to the surface.

If she had been made of stone, she would have plummeted to the depths, igneous and dense. But lungs clamour for air, and a woman's belly and thighs are succulent with fat, which floats as oil does on water.

If only Archimedes of Syracuse, the Greek inventor and physicist, had been at that riverbank to explain buoyancy to these marauding hordes. Would his explication have absolved her or changed the minds of her rampaging accusers? We can never know, for even though he had been dead for many years, his inventions had not reached the hamlet. If only the predatory masses had realised that the weight of a body in water changes due to the upward thrust of liquid against it.

If only King Ferdinand's men had known about water displacement, perhaps science could have displaced suspicion. Then perhaps the compassion of a boy once called Luciano and renamed Lazaro de Abismo might not have sunk on that orphaning day.

Inez had not wanted a child fathered by maliciousness and an absence of tenderness, by a brute who forced himself upon her. But yet, Luciano came. His birth had been a punishment for her. He had been unable to tumble head over heels in her womb so he might come out headfirst as babies know so well to do. After many hours of desperation, Inez had cried, 'Get this child out of me!'

She had come, as she always did, when a woman called her name: La Primera de los Ojos, the midwife. It had been one of the cruellest births, beset with panicked intervals when she feared she might lose both the mother and the child. But she whispered pleas under her breath, and rested wet cloths on the poor mother's forehead, and pressed her elbows on the woman's belly to try to turn the child. She sang gentle upside-down tunes and songs of the somersaulting starlings to calm the mother and coax the child. None of her tricks worked.

At last, when the mother was almost unconscious from the effort, she reached in and grabbed one of the infant's legs in her hand. She did not want to, you must believe this, but she had no choice. She broke it once, and then twice, so that it became a floppy lever, and with it she was able to pull the rest of the baby free.

Luciano lived, but a part of him died in his birth.

Chapter 25

When Teo opened her eye, it was morning, and the forest was rowdy with gusts that shook the trees and swayed their branches till they creaked. She was covered in the old woman's rabbit and pine marten shawl, which had kept her warm through the night.

It was not the only sign that the old woman had been there, for in front of her lay the dark patch of charcoal where the fire had burned down. Her carved walking stick rested on the forest floor.

Teo wrapped the pelt over her shoulders and her fingers around the wooden handle of the staff, which was animal-warm in her palm. How could the old woman get far without these? She clutched the cane to her chest. To surrender friends such as these could only mean that time was running out, for this is when things pass hands. They were Teo's to take care of now.

Teo spied Isabel sheltering beneath bushes, in all likelihood to protect Patito from being whisked away by the wind. Her scrip, no longer weighed down by the fork, had been carried off a distance. Teo discovered it stuck between a log and a rock.

Teo then gathered her companions.

Despite Patito's reluctance, she grasped her firmly and enclosed her in her scrip for safekeeping, apologising as she did. 'It's for your own good,' she consoled, 'which is also The Greater Good, for Isabel and I would not wish to lose you.'

Her thoughts ran to Sancia. Her fever. Her papa. His bravery. Her fork. It was gone – the old woman was taking it to Malakha in exchange for a miracle.

'Please let it not be too late,' Teo whispered.

At this point in our story, we might expect Teo to return home as fast as she could, to avoid the storm. Instead, she and Isabel quickened their pace and hastened far and furious for many hours, until the forest ended and the beach beckoned. Teo followed her nose, if only to finally behold it, at last, with her very own eye.

It spread out in front of her, a foreverness of water, glinting with a million winks, whipped by the wind and curdled with currents. The water crashed to the shore in exhilarating thuds, foaming and swirling against the sand.

Was this the sea that had swallowed her mother? Her *mother*? Who was her mother? For all the time she'd been missing her alongside Sancia and her papa, the truth was that she had never known Gracia. The beekeeper Valentina? She had not a scrap of memory of the one who had carried and borne her.

In the orbits of imagination, a fear may churn with ghosts and myths, looming larger and more hideous than the thing on its own terms. But in the grounded realms of time and the end of time, a phobia might snap, as a bubble pops, leaving the chance for a new story about that thing to begin.

This is what is happening to Teo now.

Two stories – one inherited, one embodied – tussled inside Teo's heart. The scent of seaweeds and dulses called to her, the smell from her dream. Her papa's words resounded in her ears, *Never go near the ocean.* Had she promised? Was she about to break an oath to her father, who had surrendered himself for The Greater Good? Even though he was a liar about matters relating to eyes and fishhooks?

Isabel was filled with no such reservations. She trotted straight towards the shore.

Lured by a force she could not explain, Teo closed her eyes and whispered, 'Forgive me, Papa,' before she took a deep breath and, her wooden staff making first contact, she stepped onto the sand.

In the wildness of the wind, Teo walked towards the edge of the ocean. Her eye scanned the shimmering expanse. Had she ever seen such mighty beauty before? How it filled her with a longing finally met.

Everything mothers you, the old woman had pledged.

The wind gathered strength, and large clouds began to swirl above them. She had come all this way, and now, for the first time, she had an inkling of why.

Something out there was waiting for her.

The blue whale had finally made his way back to the bay of his birth. Beneath the water, he could feel the storm that was incoming. From deep within the colossus of his body, he clicked and whirred, echolocating sounds that resounded through the waters, far and wide.

'Do you hear that, Isabel and Patito?' Teo asked, her fine ears straining.

She squinted at the horizon, struck by an atmosphere so overwhelming that she could barely breathe. If she had words for what she knew, they would have been these: 'Something is about to happen. And it is a miracle.'

If we could pause the story, this is where we'd do it. All the meanderings up to now have led us to this moment.

On the forbidden beach where she stood, Teo saw it with her single eye. Isabel saw it too – a sight so improbable as a cetacean Goliath, breaching the water to inhale its last breath. It rose in slow motion, up, up. With its monocular vision, its eye facing the shore caught sight of a small human and a goat before it collapsed with an almighty splash back beneath the hurtling waves.

With this terminal bounty of oxygen in the gigantic casks of his lungs, the whale offered his final song back into the ocean. By the licences of storytelling, we might imagine that whales remember in mysterious ways, both intricate and vast, and so perhaps this was the same song he'd sung into Gracia's lifeless body, the one he'd released as he nudged a skep to shore, replete with all the complex patterns of all the sounds he had ever sung before.

This was his dying song.

All at once, Teo felt Malakha near, right beside her on the beach.

She wasn't a terrifying, gobbling monster, but a light, a refuge, a shepherdess of endings. On that windy beach, Teo felt all the sorrows she had never mourned, and they poured down her cheeks in salty streaks. A person, it seems, may grow from one age to the next not only by the markings of a calendar but in the presence of extraordinary events they know to be so.

Suddenly, she fumbled in her pockets and removed the note that Sancia had given her. She had promised not to read it, hadn't she? But since she had made that promise, everything had changed. Nothing was the same anymore. She wasn't the same.

Was Sancia still breathing? Was she still alive?

Her fingers atremble, she unfurled the note.

There, on the sand, the sky wide above her, she read it:

WE ARE NOT BLOOD SISTERS.
YOU CAME FROM THE SEA.
FORGIVE ME,
I WANT YOU TO LIVE.
SANCIA

'Oh, Sancia,' Teo called out. 'You have sent me on a wild duckling chase. You have banished me from taking care of you, in the moment of your deepest need. You are my sister, no matter by blood or by love.'

The winds began to howl around them. The sea began to whip and churn. Gota Fría was almost upon them.

It was time to return home.

Chapter 26

Graviel Torrero made sure his daughter was asleep and that there was ample wood should Taresa awake and find the fire low. A mighty storm was gathering. It was the perfect time for an undercover operation.

To mark the second celebration of their marriage, Taresa had repaired him that night with a meal of tender dumplings in a broth of chicken feet and giblets. At milestones such as these, the once intoned integrities of the past revert for recalibration. Graviel was not a sentimental man; even less might he be able to spell *sentimental*. The few words he uttered, he stood by. On this day, two turns about the sun ago, he had made a vow to honour his wife.

Honour. What did it ask of one? Of what deeds was it made? How did it present itself? And who was the judge? When every breath is a mighty endeavour, a diligence of quietening physical agony, perhaps the length of one's days bears no weight to its worth, as long as we have made good on the promises we have spoken. Graviel had lived long enough to taste the sweetness of life with Taresa by his side, and Beatris between them. Anything more was unmerited excess.

Graviel draped himself in a long dark cape, and he let himself out the door. He knew what he was about to do was treason. Despite all his misgivings, he saddled his horse and headed for the woods.

Shems slept the deep sleep of the wearied, his exhaustion stronger than any hunger. So he did not hear the knock on the door when the moon had been eclipsed by the clouds and the winds were pounding. In his dreams, he thought he heard knocking, until the knocking became a banging.

'Let yourself in,' Shems called, imagining it was Rodrigo returning home.

The banging continued.

Shems groaned and rolled over, pulling the sack of hay he used as a pillow over his head.

But the banging got more frantic. Somewhere in his dreams, he heard, 'In the name of the Marquis, open up.'

This time, Shems' eyes popped open wide.

Wrapping a coarse blanket around his shoulders, Shems sat up and mumbled, 'Who goes there? A gravedigger needs his sleep.' He finally made it to the door and thrust it open.

There, standing in the moonlight, was a looming figure wrapped from head to toe in a cloak. Shems recognised the shoes. It was one of the Marquis' men.

'We have paid our taxes,' Shems mumbled toothlessly.

'Forgive my waking you at this hour, but I need your help,' came the voice. 'Sir.'

Shems, you understand, had lived life in which scorn adhered to him like mud to a shoe. Not only was his job lowly and cursed, inducing the heebie-jeebies, the jitters and the dread of the dark dungeon of the afterlife, but his dental condition repulsed even the poor. For there is poor, and then there is poor and toothless. People never referred to him by his first name. They called him Halevi or the Toothless Gravedigger. His wife, Josefa, had been the last one to use his real name: Shems. But never in all his days, the wretched and the only slightly less wretched, had he been called *sir*. Never had he thought of himself as one who might be addressed as *sir*.

When someone who has been downtrodden all of his days on the earth hears himself referred to by a title that bestows honour and respect, a small adjustment takes place in his spine. He stands more steadily. The weight of his hours sits less heavily on his frame. He forgets that he has gums bereft of molars and that he buried four children, seven women and four grown men just hours before.

'Who calls me sir?' Shems asked, with less of a mumble.

'I come on a secret mission. Will you help save a brave man who has sacrificed himself for The Greater Good?'

'Save a man?' Shems, in all his years, had never saved a life. He had only ever been called upon when life was no longer for saving. All the fugitive yearning for the work of his days to mean something rose in him. And without knowing more, he simply nodded.

In his cell, Merdocai found himself in a prayerful daze.

He chanted to the moon he imagined was out, though he could not tell what time of day it was deep in the dungeon. He called upon the spirit of Gracia de Luna and asked her to watch over their girls.

He spoke aloud about the day Teo had come into his life, the same day he had lost Gracia de Luna. Not that she was replaceable, but a child in need is a gift to a man who is struggling to find a reason to go on.

He recounted to the cockroaches how she'd been howling, her one eye swollen from an infected bee sting. To the mice, he described the days of wrapping the child's eye in a bandage, and the seawater he used to keep it clean. He shared with them his amazement at the old woman who seared the fork in fire and then speared the dead eye, plucking it straight from her socket. *For else she might have died.*

To the rats, he confided about the rumours in the village of a witch's girlchild, which had not drowned but floated, and how fear had overtaken him. 'How could I keep her safe? I did what any father would have done,' he wailed. 'I hid her. In plain sight. A boy, not a girl.'

Suddenly, in the midst of his final confessions, he heard the sound of footsteps. Was it that time of day already? His uneaten slop stood in pails at the door. The stench would have been overwhelming had he not grown accustomed to it. He was getting weaker by the hour. He wondered how much longer he would be able to go on. Hunger consumed him from inside.

'Hello, my name is Merdocai …'

'Beneviste,' he heard a voice say.

'What is happening?' Merdocai called.

This brave man who had given himself up for The Greater Good heard words that cleaved his heart like an axe to a tree trunk.

'It is time for you to die,' the voice replied.

Graviel Torrero and Shems Halevi carried Merdocai Beneviste out of the dungeon in a coffin that Shems had made. In his weakened emaciation, Merdocai lay as still as a lifeless thing.

Remembering all he had learned from the cockroaches, he flattened his body into the minimum version of himself, enough to slip through the tiniest crack. He exhaled so completely, his lungs almost collapsed. With closed eyes, he surrendered.

'Play dead,' is all Graviel Torrero told him.

'I have died a thousand times in the past days,' Merdocai whispered.

This is how it happened that, when the morning came, without being summoned, Graviel Torrero conveyed to the Marquis the events that had transpired in the night. At the hour of feeding, when he'd taken the slop down to the dungeon, there he'd found, much to his surprise, the Subject Matter cold and dead on the cell floor. The cockroaches had already gathered in anticipation of a feast. He further recounted that, at an ungodly hour, he'd called upon the Toothless Gravedigger to fetch the body and bury it before the light of day, before questions arose.

The Marquis' lips pursed to learn this news. One of his eyes began to twitch.

'How dare the Subject Matter have the gall to expire when the experiment had only commenced. A weakling!' Spit flew from the Marquis' lips and landed on Graviel's lapel.

Graviel nodded. '*Sí*, a weakling.' As the word left his mouth, Graviel recognised that a word spoken can mean the opposite of itself, and how, finally, he was a man who could say *weakling* when he meant *hero* and keep the quiet connotation all to himself, a secret no-one could wrestle from him.

'I cannot fail. My plans cannot come to naught!'

'Perhaps ...' Graviel began, this time without losing hold of the reins of his speaking, directing it carefully, like a man with an intention, '... we have learned something from your *excellent* experiment ...' In Graviel's mind, he turned the word excellent over and saw its true face, *cruel*.

The Marquis squeezed the bridge of his nose. He was both nauseous and hungry. His head pounded. A pain tore down his left arm. Why could he not swallow?

'What have we learned?' the Marquis asked. Even now, depleted to his lowest depths, he could not resist the sweetness of a compliment.

'... that a man cannot survive as a cockroach.'

The Marquis narrowed his eyes, as if to see Graviel clearly. Lazaro de Abismo gazed at the giant before him. Something undeniable was altered in his disposition. It was revealed by a fraction in his tone, tuned marginally in his manner. Why, he seemed even taller than before. Finally the man's demeanour matched his physique.

And it terrified the Marquis.

Chapter 27

Overnight, Lazaro de Abismo tossed and turned in his lonely bed. Night no longer subdued the hamlet. The desperation beyond the citadel was undulant and festering, a maggoty mass rotting his power. It thrummed in his inner ear, a high squeal behind his eye sockets. Desperation needed a distraction, malcontent called for misdirection, before it turned to revolution.

He was running out of options. It was time to find a true scapegoat.

The next morning, bereaved of slumber, he summoned Graviel Torrero.

'Find me a witch. Scour the forests and the beaches beyond, for that is where these sorceresses hide. No swimming for her, instead we will flay her to a pulp in the public square. Dante will have first pickings from her pulsing flesh. Two birds with one stone.' His voice crackled with a hideous thirst.

Graviel, for the second night in a row, had not enjoyed more than a minute of sleep. With the storm coming, the baby had cried unendingly. He had wrapped Beatris in his cloak and strapped her to his chest and taken her into the darkness to permit Taresa some needed rest. It had been the first time he had been all alone with her, a man and his daughter beneath the night sky. The motion of his body stilled her and soon her crying eased. No matter what else befell him, or her for that matter, it would always be the case that he was the one who had shown her the stars for the first time. It was something he had done all by himself, without instruction or a plan. It had simply happened as he traipsed the streets with his bundle, noting how the orbs of her eyes had shone like polished onyx. Without any schooling, he had known what to do.

Something transmissible had swirled in him, though he did not have words for this understanding. If he had been a poet, like Rodrigo, he might have imagined himself the calyx, and she the bud. Soon he would fall away, and she would bloom ahead. This is how a man, gentle by nature, ruthless by nurture, came to his senses and perceived that his days had been more than just a worthless, aching rattle of bone on dust, an obsequious pandering to another's homicidal cravings.

It is impossible to scientifically decrypt the mysteries of how a mind changes once and for all. It was enough for Graviel to understand, as he returned home that night, that he was not the same vassal who had followed directions even earlier that day. Something true had taken hold of him, which is why when the orders of the Marquis came, they landed far away from where he now stood.

Ten years ago, long before the pox, the Marquis had commanded him to find the evil hag who had broken his leg with her clumsy hands. How could Graviel have foreseen that by bringing La Primera de los Ojos before the Marquis, he was delivering her to a ghastly fate – one that surpassed all the cruelties of war he had witnessed with his own two eyes?

Imagine poor Graviel's despair as he had stood, uselessly, to the side, his head bowed as the Marquis offered her a gangrenous choice: lose both her hands or both her eyes.

'Perhaps ...' Graviel had murmured, but the Marquis had not heard his mumblings. He had tried again. All that escaped his lips had been a small, strangled cry.

The old woman heard the garrotted sound that choked free from Graviel's throat. She turned to look at him in a brief blink, devoid of blame.

Looking her tormentor in the face, she had chosen to lose her eyes, uttering these words: 'Mine were the first eyes to see you. Now you are the last I will ever behold. You are forgiven, child. For I was there when you took your first breath.'

'Silence, Witch.' The Marquis had scowled, ordering Doctor Ignacio Tramposo to scour her eyeballs with acid, blinding her instantly. She cried out in pain as the light and colours and images of the world she had loved and cared for vanished forever. Instead of tears, blood streaked her cheeks.

'Now, we are even,' he hissed. 'Justice at last. Two eyes for a leg.'

The Marquis ordered her banished to the forest, where in her helplessness she'd be an easy feast for the bears and the wolves. But such errors of revenge do not, as we learn, set the dials of justice back to equilibrium, much as those who pursue them believe it to be so. They only harden wounds and revive the spiral of suffering, spinning it into the world for future generations to endure.

And what of those incumbents like Graviel Torrero, forced to witness such acts of inhumanity? Ruthlessness either feeds an appetite for brutality, or it causes a rupture in the soul. Ever since then, Graviel Torrero had been walking around with a fracture inside him, into which he often felt he might fall.

After the Marquis had departed on horseback, in a flurry of dust, Graviel had wrapped the old woman's head with a hempen shawl and lifted her onto his horse, Sombra. Unable to speak words of comfort or find the language to ask her forgiveness, he had ridden with her into the forest. He travelled far from the beaten track, over moss-softened rocks, through oak clusters and elm thickets, and set her down close to a stream. Before he left her, he had pressed his wooden staff into her hand.

'Let this be your eyes,' he'd said.

But now, a decade beyond that dastardly injustice, in the face of orders to once again find a witch, the ground under Graviel's feet shifted, and the fault beneath him corrected itself. With the starry sky in his heart, and his daughter's eyes in his mind, he sent the soldiers to the west and set off to the south. He knew exactly where to find her.

La Primera de los Ojos stood at the cliff's edge, where the winds were gathering. The approaching storm rumbled above. From afar she heard Sombra's hooves. It had been that beast's strong, lithe body that had carried her into the forest many years before. She could still taste the wind on her face in the endless darkness inflicted on her, which she had come to love for its own mysteries. She recalled the warmth of Graviel's body against her and his strong arm around her, his heart beating wildly in his chest. But mostly she remembered the sobs that shook themselves into her as they cantered away from the place in which her eyes had been taken.

The old woman lifted her skinny arms to the sky and welcomed the thunder and lightning and all the rain it held, like a yearning. Far out at sea, she heard the sigh of a whale that was taking its last breath.

'Ah, blessed parting,' she called into the tornado.

A bank of clouds gathered above her, rumbling and clattering.

Far below, on a beach she was forbidden to venture onto, a young girl dressed as a boy cast her longing to the wind. 'Send me a miracle. If there is an ear in the sky, please, hear my plea. Save my sister, Sancia.'

Those words climbed onto the wind, and were carried up, up, up and into a current of air that was travelling straight out to sea. They dissolved like salt in hot water into clouds that were gathering, and dispersed into them, pelting onto the ocean, where a blue whale with his finishing tremors of life sang his last song.

Right then, he released his last breath.

As he exhaled, his huge great heart stopped beating.

And

so

begnan

the whalefall.

Not all endings are made of grief.

Some are windfalls and godsends.

An ectoplasmic explosion that enriches life beyond the life extinguished.

All this happens just as an old woman, thrust into endless night, takes a sightless step closer to the edge of the cliff and Graviel's horse whinnies to a standstill.

She holds a fork in her hand and lifts it to the sky as lightning flashes.

Graviel calls out, 'Wait.' But it is, in the manner of stories, too late.

What did Graviel see? What can one man take in with his two small eyes, his aching body and tormented heart desperate for forgiveness? Only the parting of clouds, a crack of light breaking through and a figure slipping sideways into the oncoming storm.

Graviel would replay these moments over and over in his mind in times to come. She was there one instant, and the next she was gone, as if she had been swallowed by the air. He would spend the rest of his life wondering about this enigma, and each time he did, just for the briefest moment, something unfathomable flared inside him, effacing all hurts, like a bird finally breaking the spell of its captivity and claiming the sky like a prayer.

Chapter 28

At the moment of this chapter's commencement, more or less eleven years before Teo's story began, it was already late afternoon and the shadows were elongating to touch each chimney, fence and wall with their long, grey fingers. A young woman hurried through the streets, clutching her swollen belly with one hand and dragging a handwoven wicker contraption with the other. Were it a usual day, Valentina might have slowed down to watch the buildings turn tea-stained as the sun sank, but this was not a usual day.

Valentina could feel her baby was coming. It was a girl, of this she was quite certain, for she had dreamed her long before she had grown from the size of a walnut to that of a watermelon. It was enough that the Marquis knew she was with child and had sent his troops to find her. Had there been a moment to pause to consider her options, she might have; but, alas, there was no time.

How could she become a mother? Could someone, anyone, please show her? How, when the father of her unborn child – her Diego – had been killed in one of King Ferdinand's battles just weeks before? How might she look into the face of this child only to see her beloved's high forehead, the curve of his cheekbones, the exact outline of his lips mirrored there? How could she, no more than a girl herself, protect her daughter from the wickedness of the Marquis?

'It is my fault,' she sobbed as she ran, staggering on the cobblestones. 'All my fault.'

Why some people embrace guilt for situations they have not caused is a tricky sleight of human nature. It was surely not Valentina's doing that Diego had been sent to the front of the battlelines by none other than the Marquis. Why so should Valentina blame herself for his death? But ah, the human spirit, especially in the young, is a tangle of hauntings and humiliations, a muddle of sense and nonsense. If ever you have wondered why some must abide a life of Methuselan lengths, perhaps it is for times like these, when those bereft of years are in need of such elders, possessed of the vista of a long life, with eyes like the octopus or the whale to see things not as they appear, but as they really are.

With no-one to confide in, Valentina was hopeless. She and Diego had planned to marry, just as he had been whisked off to war, a four-month baby brewing in her belly.

It is time to reveal that Diego was Lazaro's half-brother, not by birth or blood, but by bad luck. Diego's mother, the previous Marquis' daughter, Marquesa Renata, had bled too long during his birth, and was advised never to risk bearing another child. So when a little orphan with an afflicted leg was discovered lost and alone in the woods, she had taken him in, filled with pity, hoping the foundling would be a brotherly companion for her Diego.

What we glimpse in a child is not the full story of what he has suffered. Torments live hidden in clenched knuckles and silent famines. The little boy could not speak his name, no more than an 'L ... L ...', so she called him Lazaro; thus his birth name, Luciano, was lost and fallen from him ever after. She raised him with reassuring affirmations that his halting leg would not hold him back, that he was smart and full of promise. Lazaro had gulped greedily from this kindness, which fermented like sugar in the silent yeast of his rage.

But no matter how evenly the Marquesa spread her love between her sons, it was never enough for Lazaro. When food was divided equally between them, he demanded more than his half-share, erupting in rages like mini storms. Whatever Diego got, Lazaro coveted. When their mother wasn't watching, he would torment his brother by laying traps of horse manure and stealing his hard-earned treasures. When Diego complained, Renata implored him to take pity on Lazaro, for he had come from such hurtful circumstances. So Diego in his gentleness overlooked, ignored, acquiesced and conceded when it came to his bullying sibling. None of this appeased Lazaro, for it is not possible to slake an insatiable hunger.

At the time of this chapter, Valentina was only seventeen, yet since she was a youngling she had lived in kinship with winged things: butterflies, moths, dragonflies and, most beguilingly, bees. She pursued them from flower to flower and then to their hives. With time and patience, she taught herself to milk honey from their combs. It was a feat of dexterity and restraint not to take too much or get stung senseless. What were a few painful welts for the bounty of honey? She only mourned the bees that gave their lives to protect their treasure. She sold the honey in clay pots at the market, where apothecaries, tincture-makers and chefs of the wealthy bought her wares for the making of medicines and the baking of cakes and sweet breads.

Here is where she met Gracia de Luna, who bartered oysters for honey to add to her daughter's milk.

Here is where Valentina's plan was devised.

Here too is where Diego had first seen her.

She let him taste a mouthful before he bought a jar. He paid her double her asking price and he left with the smell of fruity floral nectar on his lips, unable to think of anything but her. He returned again, and again, until she promised to show him the beehive she had woven from straw, where bees made their own hives.

When Valentina had shown him the honeycombs, it became his mission to craft her protective clothing: a hood and tunic of leather, so she would never be stung again. Here and with her is where he laid his life and plans.

When the Marquesa died, she bequeathed the title of Marquis to Lazaro, for Diego had no desire for power and prestige, simply a life of small virtues with Valentina.

As Diego's happiness grew, so did Lazaro's jealousy.

Perhaps all it takes is one moment for a fissure to erupt into a ravine. A man stalks his brother, only to witness an affection he has never known. It was when Valentina wet her fingers with her mouth and wiped charcoal from Diego's cheek that the scar tissue of his mother Inez's touch burned on Lazaro's own cheek. He coveted what Diego had, but he had no way to seize it.

When King Ferdinand demanded troops for a battle, the Marquis dispatched his own brother to the frontlines.

Before he left, Diego had warned Valentina that if his brother ever found out that he had a child, he feared it would be in grave danger.

As she ran through the streets, dragging the handwoven wicker beehive she had reinforced with wax to make it waterproof, she wept at the tragedies she had endured, and those still to come.

She had to find La Primera de los Ojos to help birth her baby girl.

And then, like a mother merganser, she knew what she had to do.

She would time it exactly when the woman with her fork went collecting oysters.

The birth itself had been simple. Valentina's body opened like a pod, and the little thing had glided softly into the sturdy hands of the one who had seen it all. With a tuft of saffron fluff on her head, she had gulped in the air and sung her crying song. But even as she tied the birthing cord and urged the placenta to follow in the infant's footsteps, the old woman held deep qualms, as if Gota Fría agitated within her.

Between contracting bellows, Valentina had begged her to retell her the story of the baby in the bulrushes, not once, not twice, but over and over again, through the lulls of each contraction. The old woman wondered about the labouring mother's repeated requests and grew suspicious at the intended use for the skep. Her wizened eyes had seen most things, but not all.

Imagine, if you can, the splicing of the spirit in holding a beloved child, only to know she is not yours to keep. Can we apprehend the precious hours in which Valentina held and nursed her newborn, and the madness that must have taken hold of her to execute an operation of such jeopardy, knowing it to be the only chance of her daughter's survival? For there is no-one in their right mind who would stand at the lip of the ocean and entrust priceless cargo to its hazardous might, before turning and fleeing into the forest, not knowing where or how far, but simply to outrun the consequences of her deed.

La Primera de los Ojos never doubted a doubt when it came upon her.

This is why she had secretly followed Valentina down to the ocean.

Chapter 29

Lazaro de Abismo pushed aside the glazed dish of wild boar roasted with wild garlic and forest thyme that his chef had prepared. A seasickness surged in him as if he were shipbound. His stomach heaved.

'Take this away,' he snapped. '*Déjame en paz.*'

'*Ciertamente,* Muy Ilustre Señor Marqués ...' Graviel Torrero lifted the elaborately adorned plate, loaded with succulence, saluted and took his leave for the night. A man might live in hope for many long hours on his feet to hear the command, 'Leave me in peace.' When at last it came, it dispatched him to freedom and relief. But peace did not come to the Marquis.

It had not eluded Lazaro de Abismo's attention, the nearly imperceptible lilt in the corporeal acreage of Graviel Torrero's *latissimus dorsi* as he turned and exited the chamber. The Marquis closed his eyes and tried to imagine the notion of *returning home*, where another might be waiting to receive one, in all one's discomposed dishevelment. This day and the many days that preceded it broiled inside him. His throat burned with bile. His bowels cursed and groaned. Sleep shunned him entirely, overborne by the relentless hunt of his mind. He could not repress the plummeting nor master the act of swallowing.

What if, he daydreamed, in the besetment of turmoil, a soft hand might brush one's unshaven cheek? How might it be to tumble into an embrace in a kingdom far from the insurrections of ineptitude and the chaos of disorder? The inheritance of his undeniable poverties suffocated him. With all manner of wealth at his fingertips, he felt throttled by the injustice of all he did not have.

Lazaro de Abismo felt his forehead. It was blazing.

He grasped his chest. It was tightening.

He opened his mouth to take a breath, but it was as if he were drowning in air. He broke into a cold sweat. A ghastly pain screamed down his left arm.

'Help,' he tried to call, but it came out as a muted yelp. 'Help …'

The Marquis stumbled towards his padlocked chest, fumbling to fit keys into the one-two-three-four locks, gasping and breathless. Finally, they fell to the floor, *clunk, clunk, clunk, clunk*. He grabbed the bottles of elixir and drank down one, two, three in quick succession, spilling most of the precious medicine on the marble floor.

There could be so much more to say about these last moments.

Yet no-one who might help was nearby to hear his cries.

The moths drew close to the lanterns and the cockroaches danced in the corners.

Dante drooped on his perch, indifferent.

In the morning, Graviel Torrero found the Marquis' cold body curled around the trunk of elixir, his pair of once-seeing eyes wide in a terrified gaze. Cockroaches crawled over him.

'Muy Ilustre Señor Marqués.' He exhaled, in a tone bereft of irony, for Graviel was not one to trade in such word and mind games.

Standing in the Marquis' chamber, Graviel understood that he had been given a chance to live a different kind of life. He removed his tight-fitting helmet for the last time. It was as if the true blue sky had opened for him, and he could see something beyond the shadow that had crept over his life when he was sent to war and wounded for life.

He removed the blinders from Dante the albino goshawk's face. The eyes of the great bird glistened dully at him, two perfect red orbs. Dante had lived all his life in confinement, since captured as a small bird by Lazaro. An eminent predator of the wild, he had been tied to a wooden stake for all his days. He could go no further than he was trained to. He took orders in return for a mouse or rabbit fed to him by hand from his master.

But as Graviel looked him in the eyes, he saw an unassailable truth: that the endless sky lived inside him. The great mountains and oceans moved in the heart of this goshawk, a heart no bigger than a hazelnut. What a creature does not know, they say, it does not miss. But that is only if one believes that the great wilderness is *out there* and not threaded into the blood and feathers and bones and bark of all that lives.

Dante could not know what was about to happen as Graviel flung open the windows. He had no inkling of the immensity of change that awaited him. If he had known the word *destiny*, perhaps he might have uttered it in the language of goshawks as Graviel slowly released the jess on his foot. The feathered animal surveyed the almost boundless heavens, blinking with all the thoughts of things with wings; then, stretching his own as wide as a king's cape, he took off into freedom, like all wild creatures should. And into the grace of that gesture, Graviel's spirit surged.

He bent down to retrieve one of Dante's feathers and laid it on Lazaro's lifeless form before he left the chamber.

To begin afresh.

But this is not a time to celebrate. If pity resides in us, this is the moment to gather it up in our hearts, like a small bundle of fallen twigs.

People are not born evil or cruel. They learn it.

Sometimes they are hurt into it.

Let's rewind and sit beside Lazaro de Abismo as he takes his last few breaths.

He is all alone and filled with fear. He is no longer a man who commands an army and a kingdom. If we look into his heart, what do we find but a boy who wants his mama; a child who longs to be comforted in the arms of the right person, who knows how to unfrighten him and soothe him as he faces his fate. As he is dying, a man wants to know, *Will there be crying?* As he slips into the longest sleep, he longs for just one person to weep.

In the short moments in which the blood could no longer get to his heart because all the meanness of his life had snarled into a blockage, he understands it all. He has lived a meaningless life in a lonely tower. His has been an existence of vanity, built on the horrors of torture and imprisonment. He has wandered like a child through his days, in uniforms that never fit him, always trying to hide his wounded leg. His soul has withered in shame and all he has ever succeeded in doing in his life is extending his suffering onto every other living creature.

In these moments, as Malakha looms over a writhing soul, it is a well-documented fact that She arrives with a question: *With what were you smitten? To what did you give your heart?*

As much as he fought for breath, grasped for medicine and struggled for life, he could find no answer. Lazaro de Abismo had never been smitten, for to be smitten is to love, and poor Lazaro knew nothing of such a benediction. He had, if anything, been be-demoned by a lust for power, driven by fear – which is the opposite of love.

We might say that Lazaro's ending was the exact opposite of the whale's. As we noted at the start of this tale, Nature is the ultimate equaliser.

Though many cheered and celebrated when they heard the news that the gammy-legged Marquis had lost his life, Merdocai Beneviste was not one of them.

In time, he would find his way to the appointed grave and wish the Marquis' soul peace after a life of torment and tormenting others.

Later, a tree would be planted alongside the Marquis' grave. The idea had been Rodrigo's, so that someday, long after they had all been returned into the hammock of the earth, a great oak would grow there, offering shade, giving oxygen, providing homes for spiders and birds and the many creatures of the wild.

Chapter 30

For the last time, then, we find Teo, almost swept off her feet, heading back into the forest and towards her home of Vilingraz, with Isabel leading the way, to find shelter from the inbound storm.

As she crosses the sand, leaving behind two sets of footprints – hers, and the hooves of a goat – she will hear a cry above and lift her eye to see a swoosh of white wings, a goshawk, surfing the clouds.

'He is waving to us, Isabel, is he not?' she will ask. 'Yes, I am certain that he is,' she will concur with herself.

As she enters the forest again, she will hear his footsteps long before she sees him, for her clever ears, as delicate as the tympanum of the crickets, grasshoppers and katydids, recognise the sound even from many miles away. As the rains begin and the lightning shudders, Teo will not falter until Rodrigo is standing before her, a boy who has never been happier than in the moment he sees his friend has been in every way unsuccessful in finding Malakha after all. He will guide her into the lair he has built in the woods, where Teo, Isabel, Patito and he will see out the Gota Fría, with two slices of honey cake and so many stories between them that the storm seems to pass like a bad temper.

Now that she has been far away, Teo holds everything differently. She sees and hears things as they truly are. Her never-going-away dream. Her long-lost love for the ocean. One of her many mothers' honeyed name on her lips. Her encounter with Malakha, who awaits each one of us behind the curtain of life.

She has accumulated a motherless duckling along the way, who is now part of her family, as precious as a sister, as beloved as a best friend, and a wooden staff passed on from Graviel Torrero to La Primera de los Ojos, and now to her.

But it will only be when Teo, a full day later, emerges from the forest and returns to her home to set eye on her father again, his hair and beard shorn, that she will have an inkling of how deep the mysteries of the universe run. When Merdocai's gaze fixes upon Isabel's smitten passenger, he will fall to the ground and smother the merganser with kisses, burbling and bubbling with a tearful joy she has never seen in him before as he cries, 'A duckling ... oh Gracia ... a duckling ...'

Something larger than everything that has tried to break her family will flit inside her.

It is a largeness greater than small men who crush hope with fear; it outlives a fever and the bodies it leaves in its wake. It is woven from the murmurs and stutters of a friend's poetry, the smoke of a fire, the long-lost aroma of honey and the sounds of a whale's last song.

Hope is not made of the gossamer threads of Spanish moss, nor the wings of a dragonfly. It is woven from many strands, like the rope tying a girl with one eye to her trusty goat, or a skep sealed with wax to carry a child to safety. It is as old as mountains and soiled with use. It has worn many weathers, and though it is frayed, it never breaks as long as you keep holding on to your side of it.

Teo knows it, and now you do too.

But friends, this would not be a story for the ages if we insist on a hero and, most of all, a happy ending. There are no individual heroes nor endings — whether happy or unhappy. Every moment in a story is an unfolding of possibility — for who knows where it might lead?

Will Sancia survive the pox, strengthened by the honey cake, and fulfil her promise of never being afraid again? Does Shems put down his shovel and become a baker of the best breads Vilingraz has ever tasted? Will the duckling ever stop being smitten with Isabel? Do you suppose Merdocai will relocate his family back to Dazic, the village by the sea, and take up his old title of Bream Whisperer again? Will Teo go on to search through the forest for the beekeeper Valentina, the mother who sent her to sea in a skep? Will she learn the truth, that she is the daughter of Diego, the Marquis' half-brother, and will it matter? Will she grow her hair and become Dorotea, or will she live in the in-betweenness forever? Will La Primera de los Ojos ever be seen or heard from again? When and how will the pox end, and will a benevolent marquis replace Lazaro de Abismo, to bring peace and harmony back to the hamlet?

Some questions have simple answers, and others fade away into the great unsolved mysteries of the universe.

Even though it hasn't happened yet, Teo will pass the wooden staff to Rodrigo, for certain things have rightful owners while others are simply their conduits. When he holds it in his hands – can you guess? It will calm his stuttering, as if he were nestled against the trunk of a great oak, rooting him to the earth.

When we remember that we are a small part of the great aliveness of the world, no more special or grand than a goat, goshawk, duckling or whale, then all life is served. Where there is life, there will be more stories filled with love and courage, and very probably tragedy too.

For example, will Dante go on to hunt on his own terms, or will he be found by Rodrigo, a clump of perfect white feathers in the woods, having tasted freedom just once before he died? If this breaks your heart, that is okay. For stories teach us how to love, how to be brave and how to survive grief.

If there is anyone who knows how to bury a once-living thing, and by so doing, return its glory to the world, it is the son of Shems the Toothless Gravedigger, who will find a perfect place for it beneath Abuela Guardiana, the Grandmother Guardian Tree.

Now, as we come to the end of our story, we find Teo skipping through the forest, homewards, with a thousand new questions and stories fluttering inside her. Do you feel it as she does? That our world is filled with endless tales and wonders, and the end of one is just the beginning of another? This must surely be what Teo is thinking as she remembers not only her many mothers, but everything else she is woven from – the whale, the ocean of everythingness, the vast sky and all in between. She has been far away and now she can see and hear things as they truly are.

As the whale's bones begin their long sinkage to the lowest oceanic fathoms, spawning an ecosystem of life, it blesses and blesses and blesses the world.

'I remember that I was found. I remember that I was saved,' Teo whispers.

It is possible to rejoice in the breathingness of all things, the feelingness of the world, the everythingness of the ocean that threads us to the pulse of light.

It is possible if we are smitten, as Teo is, with life.

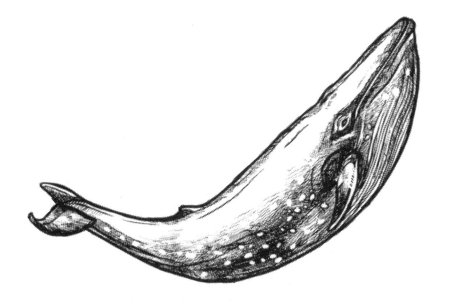

Author's Note

The Whale's Last Song slipped out of me while I was grieving the death of my mother, who died of ovarian cancer during Covid-19 at the age of eighty-one.

For many months, I was unable to function properly in the world. All I could do was lie on my bed, reading. And nothing too long or too taxing.

I came across Kate DiCamillo the children's author, bought all her books and read them one after another. I wrote the first three chapters of *The Whale's Last Song* almost immediately after finishing *The Magician's Elephant* – oh, if you haven't read it, lucky you. That joy still awaits.

The voice felt like a ventriloquism; I did not recognise it. It came from somewhere in the fathoms of my childhood. I was writing it for a little girl, perhaps the child I had become having just lost my mother. I was speaking to the part of me that had first fallen in love with writing and storytelling, when I used to read Enid Blyton's books filled with imaginative worlds that children must navigate without the help of grown-ups.

All I had was a girl with one eye, running through the cobblestoned streets with a note – and … a fork? (My friend Wiremu lost his mother when he was eight years old, and a fork is the only thing he inherited of hers – a tender fact I have cupped in my heart since he first told me.) My character's sister had the pox and she would do anything to find a cure. I had no idea what I had thrust her into, but thrust she was. And me with her.

The book is a complete departure from anything I've written in the past twenty years, in terms of genre, voice and story.

It started out as a bit of fun – could I write such a book? How ridiculous was I allowed to be? I played with the character of the Marquis (how evil could I make him?) and how absurd could I make his Genius Plan (invoking the Trumps and Putins of our era)?

I didn't know I had it in me to be so *frolicsome*.

But soon I began to take it more seriously as the characters started coming to life – every one imperfect, maimed, broken in places, but so beautiful. Shems Halevi, the toothless gravedigger; Rodrigo, the stuttering poet who loves the forest; Merdocai, who surrenders himself to be experimented on to cure the pox (like many of us did when we had our

Covid vaccinations); Graviel, an enormous, dyslexic, wounded soldier who has just become a father; and Teo, an eleven-year-old girl, who is pretending to be a boy, because her father is trying to protect her from the witch hunts of medieval times.

Every chapter took me further into the forest of this story, where I waited to be surprised by what would emerge on the page.

I hoped the story would make readers want to read it aloud, the way we long for a mother to read to us before we go to sleep. I wanted your tongue to itch to say:

'There was a time / when the forests and the
mountains / and the sloping woods belonged
to no human.
The world was a pulsing heart, /and each small thing
knew its place in this grand scheme,
without which, the whole machine of it would stop,
and all that lived, would die.'

It became a rumination on leadership and corruption during a pandemic. The evil Marquis is based on Joseph Goebbels, who was a philologist, a master of propaganda. The Marquis' language is pulled from the eugenics movement, 'scientific racism' and the belief that some people are inherently superior to others.

But it is also about family and sacrifice and intergenerational trauma and the pattern of how things fit together. Far beyond the human tragedies that are playing out is a whale coming to the end of its life. Its impending death is not a catastrophe, anything but.

I've been an open water swimmer for the past five years, since a severe back injury, and how I have become sodden and smitten with the sea. I wanted this novel to be a love song to the ocean and all its creatures. While writing the book, I listened to hours and hours of whale song, letting it infuse me. Rebecca Giggs' astonishing book *Fathoms: The World in the Whale* is where I came across the concept of *whalefall*. It holds the central metaphor of the book.

This is how the concept played out in my thinking: while we all try to live well and often fail, sometimes dying in the right way 'on one's own terms' is the only way we can become a blessing to the world. In life, we often have no control over the events in which we get caught up – I think that's obvious in our modern world, where we have 'runaway' consequences politically, environmentally, psychologically and technologically. We cannot halt or interrupt them, we are swept up, like Gracia in the waves, in a system that will take us down. So how we die, and when we die and what happens to the world after we die, is perhaps the only gift we can leave behind.

Some year ago, I was introduced to the diaries of Etty Hillesum, a Dutch writer who died in the Nazi concentration camps. I cannot shake the thought that Etty knew she was going to die and yet she still made meaning of her life, right until the end to be the 'thinking heart of the barracks'. She offered comfort to those who were suffering. She sang on the way to the gas chambers, even though there was no point, no reward, nothing in it for her. She was able to stand back from the horrors and not take the circumstances in which she was ensnared, personally. She understood that there was a greater pattern, a larger timelessness in which she was a small player, powerless and yet integrally part of it all. No matter what she did, she couldn't halt the Nazi machine. She had several opportunities to escape her death, but she chose not to. The Nazis were fixated on numbers and she knew that if she somehow slipped through the knot of fate, then somebody else would have to go in her place and she simply could not justify the idea that her life was somehow more important than anyone else's.

I've been profoundly changed by that idea, as a way to live.

In my little story, we have characters who are willing to risk their own safety to protect others or to protect a different world they will likely not benefit from. Merdocai surrenders himself for The Greater Good because he wants to try and find a cure for the pox. Sancia sends Teo away so that she won't get infected. Teo goes on the journey to try and save Sancia. Gracia sacrifices herself to try and rescue the baby in the basket. Valentina sacrifices her child to the ocean to try to protect her. Graviel puts himself in danger by trying to save Merdocai. And of course, the whale, when it dies, gives everything back to the ocean so more life may continue.

This book is also about the strange and numinous ways in which things come into our possession, and how they pass from one person to another. An object may arrive, a gift from the ocean, which has a particular meaning to us, until we hand it over to someone else, where its significance is reimagined. Or we may create something of value, which we then find reason to offer to someone else who needs it more than we do.

These objects live many, many lives. They outlast all of us. As precious or sentimental as we regard things, they can't be taken into the next life.

Books are like that. They become objects for others to pick up, bestow with their own meaning and pass on with the blessing: 'Read this.' How humbling, as an author, to be reminded that I am just one note in a great song that is singing through us all. And while this story rests in your hands, I get to be part of your song, and you, part of mine.

JOANNE FEDLER
Sydney, 2024

Spanish Terms

Teodoro and Dorotea are names that both mean 'gift from God'; one is a boy's name and one a girl's.

Absolutamente: Absolutely

Abuela Guardiana: Grandmother Guardian

Así que?: So?

Avance: Come here

Bobo grande: Big fool

Ciertamente: Certainly, of course

Déjame en paz: Leave me in peace

Diablos: Devils

Dineros: Money or cash

Dios mío: My God

Es irreparable: It's too late

Estupido idiota: Stupid idiot

Grandes idiotas: Great idiots

Idiotas indigentes: Poor idiots

!Hurra!: Hurray

Indudablemente: Undoubtedly, undeniably

La Primera de los Ojos: The First of the Eyes

Madre de Dios: Mother of God

Medico de la Peste: The Plague Doctor

Mi querido/a: My dear, or my beloved

Mia cariño: My beloved, my dear

Muy Ilustre Señor Marqués: Most Illustrious Lord Marquis

No importa: Never mind, it doesn't matter

No se: I don't know

No servirá: It won't work

Nuestra ballena bebé: Our baby whale

Perdón: Sorry, pardon

Perdóneme Doña: Forgive me, madam/ma'am

Sí, es cierto: Yes, certainly, it's true

Tía: Aunty

Torpes ineptos: Inept fools

Uno, dos: One, two

Terms I Learned While I Wrote the Book

Abditory: a secret place for hiding or protecting things of great value.

Barca: a small fishing vessel used in medieval times.

Buoyancy: or 'upthrust' is the tendency of an object to float in a fluid due to the upward force of the fluid that opposes the weight of the object.

Caprine: relating or pertaining to goats.

Conduction: the process by which heat energy or electricity moves through the atoms or molecules of a substance (usually a solid).

Enskyment: to raise in rank, power or character, to praise highly or glorify.

Gota Fría: a meteorological phenomenon in the Mediterranean in which sudden high winds and heavy rainfall occur, causing flash floods and damage to property and infrastructure. It occurs when warm air from North Africa clashes with the cooler air from the Mediterranean, instigating terrific convective storms.

Jess: a short leather strap that is used to fasten the leg of a hawk in captivity.

Merganser: a type of crested marine diving duck with a long slender bill. It is also called a 'fish duck' because it is a fish-eating creature.

Photosynthesis: the process that happens when green plants containing chlorophyll use sunlight to convert carbon dioxide into oxygen.

Rip: is a current that flows away from the shore out towards the open ocean consisting of darker water with fewer breaking waves as the water is moving in the opposite direction.

Scrip: a larger bag in medieval times, made of fabric, typically worn over the shoulder or across the body using a strap. It was commonly used by travellers, merchants and pilgrims to carry provisions, documents and other essentials during their journeys.

Skep: a dome-shaped medieval beehive. It was a basket woven from straw or wicker with a little entrance for bees to come and go. They were used to house honeybees and collect honey.

Stridulation: is the sound made by insects, such as crickets or cicadas, when they rub certain body parts together to make a chirping or buzzing noise.

Trencher: a flat round of hardened or stale bread (cut from a loaf of rye or barley) that can be used as a plate or eaten on its own. Sometimes the trencher would be eaten with the meal, or would be discarded and given to the poor or animals to eat.

Water displacement: when an object enters water, it pushes the water out of the way to make room for itself. The amount of water that is displaced is the same as its own volume. An object that displaces its own weight equal to the weight of the water will float, no matter how heavy it is.

Whalefall: when whales die, their carcasses sink to the ocean floor and provide a sudden concentrated source of food for millions of ocean-dwelling creatures and organisms for decades.

Acknowledgements

I wrote this book on the unceded Gadigal land of the indigenous Eora nation as a migrant to a country 'girt by sea'.

Each morning, I stand on Coogee Beach, and ask for permission to enter and safe passage while I'm in the ocean.

I am beholden to the Traditional Custodians of this ancient continent for their care and guardianship of Country and its waters, for their deep listening and Dreaming, which have given me the chance to know myself anew in kinship to this place and all its creatures. I do not take it as anything but a privilege and a blessing each day to return as a visitor.

For all my life, I have been touched by the wisdom, research and understanding passed on by friends, family and teachers through role-modelling, stories and books.

My father, Dov, a legendary political cartoonist, painter, sculptor and writer, instilled in me the agitation of creativity and imagination from my earliest years. Over decades we have shared the riotous joys and frustrations of being artists, with all the necessary experiments and failures. 'You're a born *tumul*,' he told me (a Yiddish word for 'commotion'). I learned that from him. He was my first teacher in the magic of making something from nothing.

I'm grateful to my Buddhist teacher Joyce Kornblatt for introducing me to the diaries of Etty Hillesum, who lived only to the age of twenty-nine, but whose insights help me daily to be a more human human.

I keep returning to the poems of Rainer Maria Rilke and the lyrics of Leonard Cohen and Nick Cave – they keep my heart open. I have grown tender and curious through the teachings of Carl Jung, Andreas Weber, David Abram, Rachel Carson, Margaret Wheatley, Joanna Macy, James Hollis, Sophie Strand, Stephen Jenkinson and Tyson Yunkaporta. I trained in warm data with the brilliant Nora Bateson, whose work extends that of her father, Gregory Bateson, in the patterns of mutual learning that exist in living systems. I give thanks for all the clever people who came before us, and who are still among us.

My beloved friend Miriam Hechtman recommended Ann Patchett's book *These Precious Days*, without which I would not have come across the children's author Kate DiCamillo.

Thank you to Kate DiCamillo, whose toes I would

kiss if I could, for her beautiful, soulful books, but most especially for *The Magician's Elephant* which is almost certainly the single inciting stir that whisked *The Whale's Last Song* out of me.

I structured the story over five April days at a desk in a lighthouse as part of a residency at the Newcastle Lighthouse Arts Foundation, a rare and generous opportunity. Here I discovered – with a small gulp – that it is only male whales that sing when all along, I had conceived my whale as female. I was so annoyed by this rookie error on my part, I almost gave up on the story. But as you can see, I pulled myself together.

I wrote this book for my grieving self, without a literary agent or a publisher. But then Lou Johnson scooped me up in her newly formed agency Key People Literary Management, and I became her and Jeanne Ryckmans' first contracted deal, in what felt like a wink. I am privileged and thankful to have Lou and also Darryl Samaraweera from Artellus Literary Agency in the UK as my brilliant champions and cheerleaders. Their reactions to the story and confidence in it brought me back into the fold of traditional publishers, where Lou scored me the Holy Grail: Catherine Milne at HarperCollins.

In 2007, Catherine Milne worked on my book *Things Without a Name* while she was at Allen & Unwin, and I have longed ever since to be fairy-godmothered by her exquisite editing and touch. I wrote the first draft as a children's book, so it was a challenge when Catherine asked me to rewrite it for an adult audience. I would never have chosen an eleven-year-old protagonist had I set out to write for grown-ups. But, like the old woman says to Teo, 'What if you came all this way to give me this fork?' It seems I had to pen a children's book first to uncover the final version. The book you now hold in your hands is the synergy of Catherine's insights and feedback with my rewriting. Please include her in any appreciation, for she is invisibly stitched into the story at every turn.

I gave the manuscript to a few early readers, whose capacious hearts billowed my sails: to Maggie Hamilton, Suzie Miller, Tanya Southey, Kirsten Garbini, Lorraine Abraham, Kerry Taylor, Mary Goslett, Graeme Friedman, my sisters Carolyn and Laura, Zed and Jess, thank you for your sighs, oohs and aahs; and the tinkling of words like 'extraordinary', 'mystical', 'exquisite', 'lyrical', 'wonderful', 'destined for greatness', 'magical', 'profound' – yadda-yadda. A book, like a child, needs early unconditional love and you were all generous with yours.

To those who worked on the edit – my wonderful editors Rachel Cramp and Rebecca Sutherland, I appreciate how fastidiously you loved the manuscript into shape and your careful eyes on the text, knowing that to me, every single word matters.

I am moved by the inclusion of some of my own illustrations; doodles that never imagined themselves in print, and yet, here they are, an echo of the children's story I first intended to write.

I want to hug Hazel Lam for her exquisite cover design (a huge 'yes' leaped from my chest when I first saw it), and Caitlin Toohey and the HarperCollins marketing team for all their quiet but powerful work in the underswell, for being the tide that takes a book from my heart to a reader's.

I have so much love and appreciation for Jane Turner, from my favourite bookstore, Gertrude & Alice, for her unwavering support over many years, and her genuine delight and anticipation of this book.

Thank you to Zed (again) who goes into the office so I can stay home and write; and for his dogged belief in this madness I call my 'work'.

When my offspring and their partners sit around my dining room table, I am overcome with the grace of belonging – it is what everyone in this story aches for. 'Never happier,' Zed nudges. That is true (except perhaps when I am swimming).

I could not do very much writing without sleep, a roof over my head and food on my table – the gifts of so much random privilege and luck. Sometimes I am bewildered and awed by all I have been given, which includes Archie, our cat, who sits beside me while I write and only nags at 4 pm when it is his dinner time.

I am grateful to McIver's Ladies Baths and Wylie's Baths where I have spent many hours swimming and writing. Jacques Cousteau wrote, 'We protect what we love.' Swimming has brought me face to face with so much precious marine life, and grown my love of the sea and everything that lives in it. To Sea Shepherd, the Australian Marine Conservation Society, the Great Barrier Reef Foundation and all individuals and organisations working to protect our oceans – thank you, thank you, thank you.

To the stranger who left two heart-shaped rocks in Coogee Bay (one carved with the word *FRIENDSHIP*, the other with *CREATIVITY*), which I found on my swims while writing this book: you gifted me mystery and numinosity just as I called to the sky, 'Send me a sign.' You will never know how profoundly you touched my life.

And to my mama, Dorrine, wherever she is now – who, in her dying days, said to my father, *I love my life*, a tattoo that is now inked on my left forearm in her handwriting, thank you for the whalefall of your dying, of which this book is a fragment. You live on in Teo, who is smitten with Life. I only wish you had lived long enough to read this story.

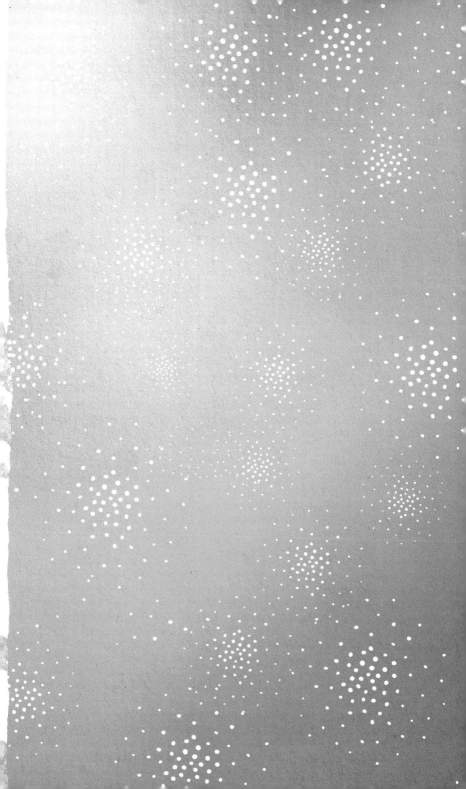